Freya suddenly  **must have bee... the same time as hers.**

The sudden shock as she tried to imagine how she would be feeling at this moment if it had been *her* lying on that bed left her brain frozen.

"Freya?"

That was Finn's voice, and his hand on her arm turning her away from the tear-stained woman to face him.

"I'll deal with this one," Finn said gruffly, his warm hands bracketing both her elbows in an infinitely supportive grip. "Go and get yourself a cup of tea before you keel over."

She looked into those green eyes and could have drowned in the ocean of concern she saw there. Instead, she stiffened her spine. "I'm all right," she insisted. "I just need to—"

"You just need to do as you're told," he interrupted firmly.

Surprise left her with her mouth hanging open for several seconds. "You're pulling rank?"

Dear Reader,

Perhaps you are driving home one evening when you spot a rotating flashing light or hear a siren. Instantly, your pulse quickens—it's human nature. You can't help responding to these signals that there is an emergency somewhere close by.

Heartbeat, romances being published in North America for the first time, brings you the fast-paced kinds of stories that trigger responses to life-and-death situations. The heroes and heroines, whose lives you will share in this exciting series of books, devote themselves to helping others, to saving lives, to *caring*. And while they are devotedly doing what they do best, they manage to fall in love!

Since these books are largely set in the U.K., Australia and New Zealand, and mainly written by authors who reside in those countries, the medical terms originally used may be unfamiliar to North American readers. Because we wanted to ensure that you enjoyed these stories as thoroughly as possible, we've taken a few special measures. Within the stories themselves, we have substituted American terms for British ones we felt would be very unfamiliar to you. And we've also included in these books a short glossary of terms that we've left in the stories, so as not to disturb their authenticity, but that you might wonder about.

So prepare to feel your heart beat a little faster! You're about to experience love when life is on the line!

Yours sincerely,

Marsha Zinberg,
Executive Editor, Harlequin Books

STRAIGHT FROM THE HEART

Josie Metcalfe

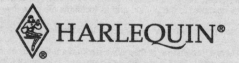

HARLEQUIN®

TORONTO • NEW YORK • LONDON
AMSTERDAM • PARIS • SYDNEY • HAMBURG
STOCKHOLM • ATHENS • TOKYO • MILAN • MADRID
PRAGUE • WARSAW • BUDAPEST • AUCKLAND

ISBN 0-373-51250-3

STRAIGHT FROM THE HEART

First North American Publication 2003

Josie Metcalfe lives in Cornwall now with her long-suffering husband, four children and two horses, but as an army brat frequently on the move, books were the only friends that came with her wherever she went. Now that she writes them herself, she is constantly making new friends and hates saying goodbye at the end of a book—but there are always more characters in her head clamoring for attention until she can't wait to tell their stories.

GLOSSARY

A and E—accident and emergency department

B and G—bloods and glucose

Consultant—an experienced specialist registrar who is the leader of a medical team; there can be a junior and senior consultant on a team

CVA—cerebrovascular accident

Duty registrar—the doctor on call

FBC—full blood count

Fixator—an external device, similar to a frame, for rigidly holding bones together while they heal

GA—general anesthetic

GCS—the Glasgow Coma Scale, used to determine a patient's level of consciousness

Houseman/house officer—British equivalent of a medical intern or clerk

MI—myocardial infarction

Obs—observations re: pulse, blood pressure, etc.

Registrar/specialist registrar—a doctor who is trained in a particular area of medicine

Resus—room or unit where a patient is taken for resuscitation after cardiac accident

Rostered—scheduled

Rota—rotation

RTA—road traffic accident

Senior House Officer (SHO)—British equivalent of a resident

Theatre—operating room

CHAPTER ONE

'BUSINESS as usual.'

Finn groaned and sighed with a combination of weariness and contentment when he caught sight of the clock above the lockers, only then realising that he'd come to the end of his shift. He raked one hand through hair that had been plastered to his skull by one of those dratted disposable hats while the other massaged the sore muscles in his back.

At least it had been worth getting backache today, he reflected with a glow of satisfaction. His efforts had been enough to stabilise the victims cut from their crushed car so that they'd survived long enough to be transferred up to the operating theatre. Not only that, but they actually stood a very good chance of recovery, albeit with a few scars they hadn't had before.

'Age starting to get to you, Finn?' challenged a husky voice from the doorway behind him and he had to fight the grin that wanted to answer the taunt. This teasing was business as usual, too, and had been ever since he'd been introduced to Freya Innes.

'In your dreams,' he retorted, turning to face the diminutive sprite standing by the partly open door, her slender curves all but hidden under the oversized green scrubs. He also had to fight his body's natural reaction to wide grey eyes filled with mischief and the heart-shaped face framed by long dark spirals that had escaped from the tyranny of a French plait—as usual.

'You haven't been at St David's a year. You're going to have to wait a lot longer if you want to step into my shoes,' he growled as he slumped onto the bench to one side of the row of lockers and leant back against the wall.

Freya gazed disdainfully down at the shoes in question, still lying higgledy-piggledy where he'd kicked them off just inside the door.

'They're not shoes…they're boats,' she declared, nudging one with a foot that was barely half the size.

'Just remember to say "Aye, Aye" when you call me Captain,' he teased, then reached automatically for the hem of his top, stripping it off in one practised move.

He paused in the act of lobbing it into the open laundry bin, surprised by the wash of colour deepening over Freya's cheeks.

Freya? Embarrassed by the sight of his semi-naked body? No way, not after all those years of medical training, he thought dismissively and completed the throw.

'So, was there some special reason you wanted to see me?' he asked, a wicked demon in the back of his mind still wondering what sort of colour she would go if he stripped off the other half of his scrubs. She'd been so easy to tease right from their first introduction, and that hadn't changed even though they'd known each other for several years now.

'Oh, nothing special,' she said with a slightly unconvincing air of nonchalance. 'I was just wondering how your weekend went. We've been so busy that I haven't had a chance to speak to you, and I wanted to catch you before you went off duty.'

'It was great.' He knew the broad smile on his face told its own story. He always enjoyed spending time with his nephews, even if it did leave him with a lingering feeling that his own frantically busy life was somehow empty in comparison to his brother's.

'Those kids are growing up so fast,' he said with a disbelieving shake of his head. 'It's one thing to learn about it in a textbook, but to see it happening in front of your own eyes... Do you know what they did this time? They waited until I dozed off in the deckchair, then tied the laces of my trainers together. Then they shouted for help!'

He scowled when he remembered the ignominious heap he'd landed in, but couldn't hold onto it in the face of her delighted laughter.

'I wish I'd seen that,' she chuckled. 'Uncle Finn felled by two five-year-olds.'

'You should have been there,' he pointed out, suddenly serious. 'Astrid said she'd invited you weeks ago.'

'You know what work's like around here,' she said with a shrug. 'Especially when you're one of the lowly juniors.'

'Surely you could have swapped shifts with someone—it was your sister's birthday after all. Your mother said it's been weeks since any of them have seen you.' He couldn't help the censure in his voice. Since his brother had married Freya's sister it had been a true joining of families, with all celebrations shared. He hadn't liked to hear the concern in her parents' voices when they'd said how long it had been since they'd seen their youngest. Now it was going to be up to him to break their news, and he wasn't looking forward to it. He'd decided it wasn't a good idea to speak to her at the beginning of their shift and had forced himself to tuck the information in the back of his mind while he worked.

'It's just the way my shifts have worked out recently,' she continued, but something in her voice didn't ring quite true and he noticed that she wasn't meeting his eyes.

Now that he thought about it, she'd been doing that for a while now, and it was something unusual in this straight-talking woman. Was she hiding something?

With a sudden pang he wondered if there was a reason why all her free time might be taken up with interests other than visiting her family. He'd been keeping a brotherly eye on her when he wanted so much more. After all this time—more than six years, and counting—was there a man in her life?

If there was, she didn't look particularly happy about it. In fact, she looked even more exhausted than he felt coming to the end of the same busy shift, and they'd both been working the same long hours for weeks. Now that he really looked at her, he could see that she looked completely bone-weary, almost as if she hadn't slept well for a very long time.

Mind you, that sort of exhaustion could have an entirely sexual reason if she was in the early throes of a passionate affair…but that was a speculation that didn't sit very easily on him in relation to the woman he'd had to force himself to think of as nothing more than his sister-in-law's sister. Somehow, he didn't want to picture the little half-pint-sized sprite in bed with any of the overgrown schoolboys and lecherous Lotharios that surrounded her in such a busy hospital.

They might not be related by blood, but they were part of the same family after all, he reminded himself hastily, totally ignoring the little voice at the back of his brain that insisted *that* wasn't why he was concerned.

Where had that annoying voice come from?

It seemed to have suddenly appeared out of the blue several months ago, not long after their mad dash to attend Max's and Matt's fifth birthday celebrations four or five months ago.

That had been about the same time that Freya had suddenly stopped calling round to his flat with an enormous pizza while they'd caught up on all the latest family gossip. About the same time that he'd noticed the elusive shadow of sadness that haunted her whenever she didn't realise he was watching her. He'd even thought once or twice that she seemed to be waiting for *him* to say something, but as he hadn't a clue what was wrong with her...

'So, how are The Parents?' she asked diffidently, using their shorthand to include both sets in the enquiry. His fruitless speculation about the timing of the change in their relationship and what had caused it was postponed indefinitely.

'As a matter of fact, I meant to tell you not to disappear at the end of the shift until we'd had a chance to talk, but...' He shrugged.

'But it's been bedlam,' she finished for him. 'No problems with any of them?'

'Actually,' he began, then could have groaned when another colleague appeared behind Freya. This definitely wasn't the sort of conversation that he wanted to start with an audience.

'Hey! None of this!' Chris Williams chided with no respect for the fact that Finn was his senior by several years as well as by profession. 'Freya, my darling, you can't ogle *his* naked body. He's your brother-in-law. If you want to ogle anybody I'm available at the drop of a scrub suit.'

'Actually, his brother is married to my sister so we're not related, but I'll remember the offer should I ever get really desperate,' Freya promised with a completely straight face, and Finn was hard put not to laugh at the comical dismay on Williams's face. The younger man had only recently joined the team and obviously hadn't looked past Freya's beauty before. He'd just discovered that she also possessed a sharp tongue.

'This is family business,' Finn said, letting the younger man wriggle off the hook of his own discomfort while he directed his next words to Freya. 'Have you got time to share a bite to eat while I bring you up to date?'

The expression in her eyes was shuttered but he had the feeling that she would have liked to have turned him down. The sharp jab of annoyance that brought him made him all the more determined that he would get to the bottom of this increasingly apparent antipathy towards him. If he had said or done something that was making her avoid family gatherings, it was important that it was resolved, especially in view of the bombshell Freya's mother had dropped on him.

'Pizza or Indian?' she offered, and he knew the choice was dictated by the two establishments she would have to pass on her way from the hospital.

'Chinese,' he countered swiftly, remembering all the goodies his mother had sent back with him at the end of the weekend. It was almost as if she still thought of him as an impoverished student rather than a fully qualified Accident and Emergency consultant. 'I'll make chicken stir-fry.'

She paused as though contemplating the offer but he recognised it for the delaying tactic it was. He also knew that she was anxious to know what he had to tell her, so he had the whip hand. At least she hadn't told him she had a hot date she couldn't break, so that was one question answered.

'I'll see you in half an hour?' she offered, knowing that the flat he lived in was one in a smart block within easy walking distance of the hospital, so that wouldn't be a problem.

'Better make it an hour,' he countered, knowing he was going to wait long enough after his shower to get a status report from surgery—not that he was going to tell her that. She'd probably use it as a reason why they should meet in the staff lounge over yet another cup of coffee.

When she looked like arguing he resorted to guile, standing up to hook his thumbs in the waistband of his green cotton trousers.

'Admit it,' he challenged, fixing his eyes on hers so that she couldn't look away unless it was to look at his naked chest. '*I* might be able to get changed and out of here in half an hour but it'll take you at *least* an hour to get yourself over to my place looking presentable.'

'Chauvinist!' she hissed as she whirled and stalked out of the door, pausing only to throw her final sally over her shoulder. 'Be prepared to eat your words with your chicken stir-fry.'

Finn was still chuckling as he braced both hands against the tiled wall and let the fierce shower pummel his aching muscles. That last expression in her eyes had been vintage Freya. If he knew anything about her—and he'd certainly learned plenty in the half-dozen or so years since their families had combined, more since she'd joined him at St David's just over a year ago—she was now racing around like a maniac just so she could prove her point.

The only question was, would she bring Key lime pie or lemon cheesecake? He knew she had express recipes for both and would take a delight in presenting one or other to him when she arrived with a 'so there' expression on her face.

Freya paused outside Finn's door to check her watch. OK, so fifty minutes was longer than thirty, but it certainly wasn't an hour, *and* she'd made dessert in that time, too.

She glanced down at herself and grimaced at the cotton sweater she'd donned after her shower. The May weather was already so beautifully warm, even this late in the day, that she could easily have worn a skimpy T-shirt—would have loved to have worn one if she wasn't going to melt—but it just wasn't an option any more.

Especially not around Finn, she reminded herself sternly, drawing on the determination that had been a constant fact of her life almost since the new year began.

Still, at least Finn's flat would be cooler than her own, tucked up under the eaves as it was. That was the price she had to pay for wanting the measure of solitude that the top of the converted house gave her. Perhaps when her salary reached the same level as Finn's she would be able to afford something as nice.

No. She drew herself up sharply when she found herself in the middle of a rerun of an old daydream. Things had changed now. Her expectations had altered over the last few months. Finn's flat was lovely and spacious but she would be looking for something smaller, preferably with access to a patch of garden.

Without warning, the door in front of her suddenly opened to reveal Finn with a teatowel wrapped around his waist and brandishing a wooden spatula.

From her diminutive height, she seemed to have to look up for ever before she found his face. Somehow she always forgot that he was at least a foot taller than she was until he loomed over her like this, his tawny hair ruffled as though he'd forgotten to brush it after he'd towelled it dry and his moss green eyes glittering with laughter.

'What are you doing, standing out here? Don't tell

me you've lost your key…again!' he taunted, then
leaned forward to sniff the concoction balanced on
one outstretched palm. 'Ha! Key lime pie! I was hoping you'd make that! I haven't tasted one for about
six months.'

He whisked it out of her grasp and strode back into
the flat, not needing her to remind him that the recently concocted dessert needed as long as possible
in the freezer until they were ready to sample it.

Savoury scented air swirled in his wake to draw
her in.

'What do you mean?' she demanded as she reached
the door of his compact little kitchen, knowing of old
not to bother entering when he was busy cooking.
There just wasn't room for anyone else with a man
of his size. 'You couldn't have known that I was going to bring that pie. I only decided—'

'—When I teased you about taking an hour to get
here,' he finished smugly. 'I was certain you were
going to try to show me up and I thoroughly approve
of your way of doing it.'

'I'm obviously becoming far too predictable,' she
grumbled as she reached around the corner to snag a
pair of place mats. 'I take it you haven't set the table
yet.'

'I saved that job for you,' he said, throwing a
cheeky grin over his shoulder.

He was a good-looking man any day of the week
but when he grinned like that he was positively lethal.

'If there was any justice in the world, he'd have a warning printed on his forehead,' she muttered as she added glasses to the table settings, tall ones ready for a long thirst-quenching drink of juice.

'How about finding a couple of stemmed ones?' he suggested from the open doorway. 'We could share a bottle of wine as neither of us is driving.'

'Um. Not for me, thanks. I'm too thirsty for alcohol.' Her brief moment of paralysis must have merely made her look thoughtful because he accepted her excuse with an unconcerned shrug.

'It won't take a minute to open it if you change your mind. Are you ready to eat now?'

The fact that they ate almost silently was a testament to Finn's cooking skills, the dish a complicated mixture of textures and flavours that was different every time he made it.

It wasn't long before their plates were empty and he brought the Key lime pie to the table.

'Set to perfection,' he said, putting it down with a flourish, almost as if he'd made it himself. 'How big a slice would you like?'

'The same size as yours,' she said with a warning tone in her voice, then wished she hadn't when he threw another of those killer grins her way.

It took a moment to get her breath back and she knew she was going to have to do something to occupy her mind. She'd found him attractive right from the first time his brother had introduced them, although it had seemed to be one-sided. When the attraction had continued to grow over the years of family celebrations, she'd actually wondered if she was making a mistake when she'd applied for a post in the same department.

It hadn't really been a problem until the weekend of Max's and Matt's birthday, since when she seemed to have been fighting an internal battle for control of her emotions.

As far as Finn was concerned, she was nothing more than another colleague at St David's, and if she wanted to be able to continue working with him she was going to have to learn to put anything else out of her mind...permanently.

'Any news on staffing levels?' she asked, knowing that their hospital was no different to any other when it came to attracting dedicated emergency care staff. Over the past few years, it had become similar to recruiting front-line troops to go into a war zone.

Unfortunately, the personnel department didn't have the same authority as an army general to deploy troops where they were most needed. At the last count their department had been three doctors short and could easily have done with nearly a dozen more nurses of all grades.

'Apparently there weren't nearly as many applicants as they hoped, and some aren't even worth calling for interview.'

'How can they tell just from a written application?

Perhaps some people will come across better in person.'

'Come on, Freya. St David's is a busy city hospital. There just isn't time to do any significant amount of hand-holding if someone isn't up to it. Anyone who wants the job has to be able to hit the ground running or the patients will be the ones to suffer.'

'I know you're right but, on the other hand, if we could take on some green recruits, we could actually train them to work the way we want them to.'

'And can you see the bean counters agreeing to pay them a salary just to stand around, watching and learning?' he scoffed. 'With more administrative staff than doctors and nurses put together, there just isn't the money for it. Anyway, with our numbers down, we just wouldn't have the time to do it.'

'So what you're saying is that it's just a vicious circle with no way out. In that case, what *are* we going to do? I know I'm one of the newer ones in the department but even I can see that the stress levels have been rising. People will only stand it for so long and then they're going to start looking for a way out.'

'It's already happening,' he sighed. 'I already know of several who are talking about going part time, or even leaving altogether. And if we can't replace them, that means those of us left here have to shoulder an ever greater burden.'

'And even more stress,' she added. 'Remember

what it was like when we had that flu epidemic back at the beginning of the year?'

'Don't remind me,' he groaned as he silently offered to cut her another piece of pie. 'Not only did we have an enormous influx of patients, but the staff were dropping like flies. Even you had to take time out, remember?'

Guilt reared its head again but Freya ruthlessly subdued it.

'I think you were the only one who stayed on your feet throughout,' she reminded him. 'Even those who'd had their flu jabs weren't completely immune because the strain had mutated just enough so they weren't protected.'

'I don't mind admitting that some days it was a case of mind over matter,' he grumbled. 'I got so tired that I completely lost track of time and kept phoning people in the middle of the night, thinking it was daytime.'

Freya could remember the teasing Finn had taken over that, and the way she'd worried about him. It had taken him several days before he'd got his head on straight again after that marathon. At least he'd been too tired to realise just how much trouble *she*'d had in getting back on her feet again.

'All right, Finn. I've waited long enough. Tell me all the news. How many messages were you given to pass on this time?' At least their linked families were always food for lively conversation, not that talking about them lessened the ache of missing them. It seemed as if years had passed since she'd seen them all. 'What other horrors have the twins been getting up to? How's Astrid? And The Parents?'

'Everyone was sorry that you weren't there,' he said, just as he had each time she'd failed to make a family get-together over the last few months. This time his voice was too quiet and there was a frown on his face that suddenly left her heart plummeting towards her feet.

'Finn?' Somehow she knew that there was something more coming than just another a guilt-inducing reprimand.

'Freya, your mother wanted us all together before she said anything, and then, when you couldn't join the rest of us this weekend, she couldn't wait any longer. She didn't want to tell you over the phone, but she had to spend a couple of days in their local hospital during the week, having tests.'

'Tests?' She tried to swallow but her mouth was suddenly parched with fear. 'What sort of tests, Finn? What's wrong?'

'Her heart's playing her up,' he said bluntly, having learned over the last half-dozen years that she always preferred bad news that way rather than sugar-coating the pill. 'Apparently, it started about a year ago but she didn't even tell your father about it until it began to get worse over the last few months. When it finally

stopped her doing her gardening your father was able
to persuade her to get it checked out.'

Freya felt sick and the room seemed to be doing a
slow waltz around her even as she gazed into the
darkened green of his eyes.

'How bad is it, Finn? What did they find?' she
demanded, her disembodied voice barely above a
whisper. Inside her head she was screaming a denial
that there could be anything wrong with her perennially active mother. This must be some sort of night-
mare. She was in her bed fast asleep and in a minute
her alarm would ring and it would all be over.

The expression on his face told her that there would
be no such reprieve. This was really happening.

'She needs surgery,' he said tersely, and it was only
when he tightened his grip that she realised with a
flash of overwhelming gratitude that he was holding
her hand.

'Surgery,' she echoed, terrified at the very idea and
yet strangely relieved that at least there was something positive that could be done. 'How extensive?'

'Triple bypass at least, and she needs it done as
soon as possible,' he said succinctly. 'It's a miracle
that she hasn't had a major heart attack already.'

'Oh, God,' she whimpered, suddenly desperate to
go home just to reassure herself that the safe haven
of her childhood was still there, waiting for her.

How could she bear it if something happened to
her mother, knowing that she'd deliberately stayed

away for so long? What if she never saw her again? Even though it had been impossible to visit, she'd drawn comfort from the fact that her parents were there, where they belonged, where they'd always been. 'Oh, Finn,' she wailed as the floodgates opened. 'She can't die. She just can't.'

Strong arms closed around her, lifting her from her seat as though she weighed no more than one of the five-year-old twins. She wrapped her own arms convulsively around Finn's neck, burying her face in his shoulder as she sobbed out her fear and misery.

'Shh, Freya,' he soothed, and she heard the familiar creak of leather as he lowered himself into his big reclining chair and settled her on his lap. 'She's seeing one of the top people in the country and he's got her temporarily stabilised on drugs. He'll look after her as carefully as if she were his own mother.'

'But Mum's n-never ill...'. she cried inconsolably. 'It didn't matter what Astrid and I got, she never c-caught it. She's always so fit and w-well.'

'In this case, appearances were deceptive,' he pointed out calmly. 'She still looks well, unless she tries to do anything physical. She must have been putting on the performance of a lifetime when she had all of us there over Christmas and New Year.'

The thought that her beloved mother had been feeling ill even then was enough to bring on another flood of tears. How could she not have noticed? She was a doctor, for heaven's sake.

'Do you want to take some time off to go down to visit her?' he suggested, handing her a handkerchief still warm from his pocket.

Her heart leapt at the idea of seeing the situation for herself, of feeling her mother's arms wrapped around her the way they always were as soon as she walked through the door... But then she remembered that the reason why she hadn't gone down this weekend still applied.

'I can't,' she wailed as the tears welled up anew.

'For heaven's sake, you can't let the fact that we're short-staffed prevent you from going to see her,' he said sternly, more than a hint of impatience in his tone. 'It should be granted on compassionate grounds or you can use some of your holiday entitlement, but that shouldn't be necessary. If you have any difficulty organising it, tell them to speak to me.'

Renewed misery flooded through her when she realised that there was no way round it—she was actually going to have to tell him why she hadn't been home in so long.

She'd put this moment off for months, knowing that his reaction could shatter her heart for ever.

She mopped her face again and blew her nose before turning her head to look up at him.

'Finn, you don't understand. I *can't* go home to see her. It would be worse for her than if I stay away.'

He frowned. 'What on earth are you talking about? She was so disappointed that you weren't there at the weekend. She actually said that the family didn't feel complete without you there, too.'

'And did she ask you if I was seeing any nice young doctors, and whether they were the sort to treat me "right"?' she challenged, knowing even before his expression changed that she'd hit the nail on the head.

'You know as well as I do how traditional she is…almost an anachronism these days. She's always seen my profession as something I'm doing to fill in the time with before I marry and have a family, and *always* in that order.'

'I remember Colum's first meeting with her, when she spelled things out in words of one syllable—terrified the life out of him, especially as he'd been hoping to share a flat with your sister while they saved up to get married.'

Freya gave a watery chuckle.

The thought that Finn's brother, even bigger and broader than Finn, could be scared of her diminutive mother had been something that they'd laughed about. But they'd all accepted that Ruth Innes adamantly refused to condone the permissiveness of modern society. As far as she was concerned, marriage came before sex, not after it, and all babies had the absolute right to be legitimate.

'Of course she mentioned it,' he scoffed with a chuckle of his own, the sound reverberating through the depths of his chest. 'You know she always does, even to your face, especially now that you're getting to the end of your twenties. She was expecting you to be settled into domesticity by now and providing her with more grandchildren to spoil. But that isn't to say that she's not proud of you and what you're doing.'

'That's why I can't go to see her,' she said softly, forcing herself to abandon the enticing comfort of his arms to stand in front of him.

It wasn't just her legs that were trembling as she steeled herself to reveal the secret she'd hidden from him for so many months.

'Finn, she might be proud of me now, but if she knew the truth the shock would probably bring on a heart attack all by itself.' She gripped the hem of her loose top in nervous fingers and drew the fabric against her body to outline the gently burgeoning evidence of her pregnant body.

CHAPTER TWO

'YOU'RE pregnant!' Finn gasped, hardly able to believe the evidence of his own eyes. Then he was struck by a savage bolt of jealousy that completely robbed him of speech.

She couldn't be pregnant. Not Freya.

He'd been watching and waiting for six years, dammit. He *couldn't* have missed his chance with her.

Ever since the first time he'd met her, introduced by big brother Colum, he'd known that she was the one he wanted...the one he'd been unconsciously waiting for while he'd played at relationships with a string of pretty women.

But he'd seen the way she'd looked at his brother and had suffered his first pang of jealousy, closely followed by the ignoble desire to have Colum disappear off the face of the earth.

Then Astrid had joined them, and he'd actually seen the moment when his oh-so-calm and controlled older brother had fallen head over heels in love.

Six years and an irrepressible set of twins later Finn was still waiting for a sign that Freya wasn't carrying a torch any longer, knowing that at the first hint that she was ready to start dating again he was going to be first in line.

And now she was pregnant?

How could that have happened?

He snorted silently when he realised what a stupid question that was. He didn't need a medical degree to know the literal answer to that question. What he wanted to know was when she'd managed to become close enough to a man to have thrown over all the dictates of her upbringing. She hadn't been working at St David's for a year yet but he already knew that she wasn't the type to indulge in one-night stands. And yet she'd obviously embarked on a relationship without a soul in the department breathing a word about the man's existence.

He desperately wanted to demand the name of the father but just one look at the mixture of shame and desperation in her eyes was enough to bring all his protective feelings to the fore.

There was an aching hole the size of the Grand Canyon inside him but the fact that she looked so perilously close to tears was the only thing that mattered at the moment. That and the fact that Ruth needed to see her daughter before her bypass surgery took place.

'How far along are you?' he asked quietly. He was being so careful not to let his own feelings show that he almost missed the flash of anger in her eyes.

'Four and a half months,' she said sharply, almost as if he should have known the answer.

He blinked and counted back, the mental arithmetic

taking him to Christmas, and he thought he understood. Had the father of her child been one of the delegates at that conference they'd attended, the sort of person who'd take advantage of the fact he was away from home to seduce a beautiful young innocent and leave her to pick up the pieces?

His blood boiled at the thought. If he'd had the man in his sights he'd have taught him a lesson that he wouldn't have forgotten in a hurry.

But vindictive thoughts weren't going to solve Freya's current problems.

Not that he had any idea what *would* solve them, he thought as he watched her blink back tears. She must have been worrying about her mother's reaction for months now. And to have the news of Ruth's cardiac problems land on top of that... No wonder she was at her wits' end.

He surged to his feet, unable to sit still any longer with a maelstrom of conflicting emotions churning around inside him.

'Have you decided what you want to do about it?' he asked as he reached for their plates and the remaining Key lime pie, unable to summon the slightest interest in finishing the last generous wedge.

'If you mean, am I contemplating an abortion, the answer's no. You might see it as a convenient way out but it never crossed my mind, not for a single moment,' she snapped immediately, and in spite of the fact that hadn't been what he'd meant, he was aware of a swift surge of approval.

'I never thought that you would,' he said calmly as he met wide grey eyes that almost snapped with the sparks they were giving off in his direction. 'You're far too much your mother's daughter for that.'

'Oh. Well, thank you.' She subsided onto the arm of a chair, almost as if she were deflating as the prickly anger left her. 'So, what did you mean?'

'Well, I know your mother wants to see you before she goes into hospital. She didn't say so, but I think she's afraid that she might not survive the surgery. She specifically made me promise to arrange for you to get a day off, preferably a whole weekend, before she goes in.'

'Finn, I can't!' She was up on her feet again, her expression reminding him of a cornered animal. 'It would kill her to see me like this. Are you sure she won't be satisfied if I just spend a long time on the phone?'

'She's your mother. You tell me,' he said simply, then continued wryly, 'We both know she's stubborn enough to put off the surgery *until* she's seen you.'

'Oh, Finn, what am I going to do?' she wailed, swiping at her face with both hands when a single tear began to trickle down her cheek. 'If I don't go to see her she'll risk her life waiting to see me, but if I do go she'll find out about the baby.'

A mean voice in the back of his head tried to sug-

gest that it was her own fault she was in this predicament. Intellectually, he knew it was his jealousy
speaking and firmly squashed it. She needed advice,
not condemnation.

'Well, I know I'm just an unobservant male, but
couldn't you just…hide it?' he suggested. He couldn't
believe exactly how unobservant he'd been for her to
have reached four and a half months without him having a clue that she was pregnant.

Even as he suggested it his eyes were skimming
over the top she'd left loosely draped over her waistband. Now that he knew what the fabric covered it
was so obvious that it existed. She'd probably only
put on half a dozen pounds or so since Christmas, but
they were all concentrated in one tell-tale spot.

'I might get away with it for a brief flying visit if
I could hide it the way I have been under a pair of
oversized green scrubs, but I'd never be able to fool
her in my everyday clothes and certainly not for a
whole weekend.'

'And you can hardly produce a husband out of the
blue, or even a fiancé to soften the blow.'

'Not without bringing the culprit with me to have
hot coals heaped on his guilty head,' she agreed, and
sighed heavily.

Finn was silent for a long time while he watched
the expressions chasing each other across her face,
knowing that she was worrying at the problem, but
there was only one question burning in his brain. Who

was the father of her child and why hadn't she automatically turned to him when she'd discovered her condition?

Or had she?

The thought that she might have been abandoned by the bastard—for whatever reason—made his blood boil all over again, and he found his hands clenched into white-knuckled fists.

With the red mist of anger clouding his vision he knew he needed time to be able to distance himself from the situation, time to get his brain working to try to find a solution. But it was time that they didn't have if Ruth was to agree to go into hospital to undergo lifesaving surgery.

Anyway, it was no business of his who had fathered her child. The fact that he was crazy enough to be insanely jealous of the man Freya had slept with was his own problem.

'Finn?'

Her soft voice dragged him out of his fruitless introspection and he realised for the first time that evening that she looked close to collapse.

'Are you all right?' he demanded suddenly, concerned for both her physical and mental state. 'You seem to have been your usual self at work but it must have been hell trying to keep something like that under wraps—or am I the last to know about it?'

She stared at him with a world of hurt in her eyes and he wondered just what he'd done wrong, then, as if she'd deliberately wiped the expression off her face, it was gone.

'Actually, you're the first,' she admitted calmly. 'Although how the whole world hasn't guessed I've no idea. There's only so much leeway in a pair of scrubs.'

He did some mental arithmetic. 'Your morning sickness was camouflaged by that second flu epidemic, wasn't it?'

'Yes. Not that I was particularly sick, apart from feeling nauseous. From what the books say, I got away with it lightly. The weight is another matter.'

He couldn't help the way his eyes slid over her, seizing the chance to catalogue every curve.

'Your breasts are fuller but your belly's hardly noticeable unless you're looking for it,' he stated, then saw the heat his comments had caused searing her face.

'Finn!' she said faintly, obviously embarrassed by what he'd said, and he couldn't help the surge of satisfaction that she'd reacted to his scrutiny.

'Still, you aren't going to be able to hide it much longer,' he conceded. 'Your body is so slim and you don't usually carry any excess weight, so the pregnancy will almost be more obvious than it would on a...plumper person.'

'Well, that's a back-handed compliment if ever I heard one,' she grumbled, then had to stifle an enormous yawn. 'That's one thing that's changed. I can sleep at the drop of a hat and my brain's absolutely useless if I don't get a solid eight hours a night.'

'But, otherwise, things are progressing well? No problems with you or the baby?'

'No problems,' she confirmed briefly, a strange expression returning to her face. Ever since she'd revealed the secret of her pregnancy it was almost as if she was waiting for him to say something, but he had no idea what it was.

Had she actually expected him to demand the name of her baby's father? It would certainly be within his role as a surrogate protective older brother. Had she been afraid that he might get on his high horse and condemn her for what she'd done? Or was she just hoping that he would come up with a magic solution that would enable her to give her mother the support she needed at this difficult time without delivering the sort of shock that might seriously hinder her recovery?

With a sigh she got to her feet, still apparently as lithe as ever in spite of her changing shape. Almost against his will he found himself wondering how her body would look in another few months when the skin would be stretched tightly enough to reveal each movement as the child shifted inside her.

It was a very short step from that to imagine how he would feel if it were *his* child she carried, his child that filled her belly with life and energy, the product of his seed that she would eventually labour to bring into the world.

Jealousy roared through him again, slashing at his heart with razor-sharp claws.

It *should* have been his child that she carried, he thought, angry even though he knew it was irrational. But he'd watched over her and waited for a sign that she was over Colum for so long that he almost felt he *should* have had the right to plant his seed in her and watch her belly grow. That *he* should have had the right to curve his hand over that burgeoning life and wait for the first fluttering signs and share the pleasure with a smile.

He escorted her to the door wordlessly, unable to find small talk, while his brain was obsessing over all the things that might have been. He knew he wanted Freya to be his, but he hadn't realised that his thoughts had been going so far in that direction—of wanting her to be the mother of his children—until it was too late.

He only noticed at the last moment, when she was stepping out of his front door, that it was now fully dark outside.

'Hang on a minute, Freya. Just let me grab a jacket and I'll see you home,' he said.

'Don't be silly!' she exclaimed dismissively. 'It's only a couple of minutes away and I've done it hundreds of times before.'

'That was when I didn't know you were pregnant,'

he said bluntly, unable to express his protective feelings any other way. 'I know it's not a particularly dangerous area but there's no point in taking chances.'

'Finn! You can't wrap me in cotton wool for the next four and a half months,' she said sharply. 'Just treat me the same way you have for the last four and a half.'

There was something more than exasperation in her tone. It almost sounded like bitterness, but it didn't make any difference to his decision.

'Willingly or unwillingly,' he said firmly as he reached into the cupboard in his narrow hallway to fish for a jacket.

Freya pulled a face but he was relieved to see that she waited. He hadn't been absolutely sure that she would. She could be utterly stubborn when she wanted to—witness the fact that she was specialising in emergency medicine when someone of her diminutive size and build could have chosen far safer options.

'Are you going to do this every day?' she challenged and he had to fight a grin. He'd known that she wouldn't let the battle of wills die without giving it another go.

'Do what?' he asked innocently, deliberately taking her arm, as she stepped down off the kerb, as though she were a fragile octogenarian.

'Hover over me,' she said through gritted teeth.

'Escort me to and from work as if I've become feeble-minded. Hold my hand in case I stub my toe on the pattern in the carpet.'

He couldn't stop the laughter this time and was relieved when she joined in. At least a healthy bout of exasperation had stopped her being so despondent.

'Dammit, Finn, you did that on purpose, didn't you?' she said with a swipe at his arm. 'I really believed you were too worried to let me walk home on my own.'

'Actually, I was. I *am*,' he admitted, and she scowled, but before she could speak he hurried on. 'Freya, cut me some slack here. I've only just learned about the baby so I'm understandably protective about you. Your family would skin me alive if anything happened to you.' He'd once hoped she'd be a real part of his family, he added silently while she digested his excuse, but that obviously wasn't to be.

'So, when you get used to the idea you'll leave me alone again?'

'Probably. In a while.'

She was still huffing her indignation when they arrived at her flat and she dug deep in her pocket for her key. When he remembered that she was going to have to climb the stairs right up to her little garret rooms up in the roof he had to restrain himself from suggesting that she ought to consider moving to a ground-floor flat. In her present frame of mind she'd throw the idea out without a second thought.

'Listen, Finn, I know you're probably still coming to terms with it, and it must have been a shock, but I'm sorry about being so crabby,' she said completely out of the blue, her slender shoulders squared with resolve and her little pointed chin up at a determined angle. 'I realise it was something you weren't expecting to hear, but I'm really grateful for the meal and the shoulder to cry on.'

Finn found himself gazing down at her with a lump in his throat, amazed at her indomitable spirit. She was no closer to solving her dilemma but she certainly wasn't going to buckle under it. Suddenly he wanted nothing more than to wrap her up in his arms and protect her from the world...but he didn't have the right. Might never have the right now, but that didn't mean that he was going to stop caring about her and wanting to see her happy.

'You're welcome, Freya,' he murmured when he'd managed to get his voice working again, then he wrapped an arm around her shoulders and pressed a kiss to the top of her head. 'Any time.'

He waited until he saw the light go on in her window before he started walking back to his flat, then decided on an extra detour through the nearby hospital grounds. He certainly wasn't ready to go to sleep yet, not with such heavy-duty thinking to do.

There must be some solution that would allow Freya to visit her mother before her surgery without breaking both their hearts. There *was* a solution, somewhere, and he wasn't going to give up until he found it.

Freya watched from the vantage point of her darkened kitchen window and saw Finn start to walk away.

She didn't need to be able to see his face to know it was him. There was only one man with that distinctive ground-eating stride and with the broad shoulders to fill that disreputable leather jacket.

It didn't take long before he disappeared from view, but in her mind she could follow every step he would take on his way back to his flat.

'You're pathetic!' she muttered as she forced herself to look away. 'Mooning after him when he's probably forgotten all about you by now.' She had more important things to do, such as make that dreaded call to her parents.

Finn had offered her the use of his phone but she'd wanted to wait till she was in her own home...until she'd regained a measure of control over her emotions.

That was a laugh. Just thinking about speaking to her mother had tears welling in her eyes. Now she wished she had Finn with her, his quiet, steadying presence unutterably comforting.

She'd expected her father to answer the call, the way he usually did, and was caught completely unprepared when she heard the soft familiar tones of her mother's voice.

'Mum?' she said with an audible quaver in her voice, the first tears already trickling down her cheeks.

'Freya, sweetheart. Don't you start crying now or you'll set me off, and your father says that's bad for me. Now, what did Finn tell you? And did he give you my message?'

Freya gave a watery chuckle. That was just so like her mother…compassionate, pragmatic, bossy and organising all by turns. The reminder was enough to give her a fingerhold on control and she was suddenly more determined than ever that, one way or another, she was going to find a way out of this mess without breaking any hearts.

'I'm sorry I didn't phone you earlier today but Finn didn't manage to get a moment to speak to me until we'd both finished working. He told me you'd finally found a way to get a few days' holiday without having to listen to Dad snore. Oh, and that while you're away they're going to fit a turbo-charger to your heart so he has to start running to keep up with you.'

She heard the answering chuckle and her spirits lifted. Somehow, the fact that she could still make her mother laugh with her nonsensical flights of fancy seemed like a good omen.

'Fitting a turbo-charger? I like the idea of that, but if they're going to turbo-charge my heart they might have to graft on a younger pair of legs,' she retorted. 'Or at least a longer pair.'

They both laughed at the perennial family joke, her father and sister taking after the tall Scandinavian grandparents on his side of the family while she and her equally petite mother were looked down on as half-pints.

'Ah, Freya, it's good to hear your voice, but when am I going to see you?' Ruth prompted gently. 'Finn suggested he could organise for you to take some time off without pay if you didn't have any days due for a while.'

Freya drew in a shaky breath and crossed her fingers, hoping for inspiration. 'Well, we have been very busy. He probably told you that we're short of staff and that means everyone's over-stretched when someone takes extra time off.'

Not to mention the fact that she was working all the overtime she could reasonably manage so that she would build up enough of a nest egg to tide her over the necessary expenses of a new baby. Maternity leave and maternity pay were all very well, but it would never be enough to make up for a full-time salary, especially as she was going to have to move house soon.

'I know, dear. I remember what the pressure was like in the early days when your father was in the same position. But, still, it's been such a long time since you've had enough leave to come home for a visit.'

Inexorable was another word that suited her

mother, Freya thought with a grimace. Bulldozer was even more accurate. Once she made up her mind about something, woe betide any one who tried to stand in her way.

'Actually,' she said brightly, 'now that I know that you're going to be in hospital, I was thinking that it might be better if I ask for time off *then*, so that I can be there to visit you each day. Of course, it would be much easier if you were coming into St David's instead of the General down there. Both Finn and I could visit you whenever we had a break up here. But that would make it difficult for the rest of the family to visit.'

Freya didn't know where the inspiration had come from but she was grateful for the delay it entailed. At least it would give her a bit longer to come up with some sort of a plan and, failing that, a cast-iron excuse for staying away. Bubonic plague, perhaps?

She could tell from the lengthening silence on the other end of the line that her canny mother sensed there was something being withheld from her. That was just one reason why, once she'd realised she was pregnant and long before the condition had started to show, she'd avoided going home. She couldn't remember a single instance where either Astrid or herself had managed to pull the wool over their mother's eyes.

'You promise?' she said finally, and Freya could have groaned aloud at the instant destruction of her

standby plan. Whatever else she may have done in
her life, she'd never broken a promise to her mother.
'You promise that you'll take several days off so you
can visit me in hospital?'

'I promise,' she said with a leaden hand clutching
at her heart, knowing that her course was now set. If
she didn't come down with an utterly genuine case
of bubonic plague, she was going to have to turn up
at her mother's bedside within the next few weeks.

When she finally ended the call her emotions were
in such turmoil that she was tempted to phone Finn,
only to turn her back on the phone at the last moment.

It wouldn't be fair. It was late and he had an early
start in the morning.

'Anyway, he's probably fast asleep by now, completely oblivious,' she muttered as she finally clam-
bered into bed, giving the pillow a vicious thump
when she couldn't get comfortable whichever way
she turned.

She wished she could just switch her mind off to
uncomfortable thoughts the way men seemed to. Still,
he'd said he would keep thinking of possible solutions
and she believed him, but deep inside she knew that
there was only one solution that would make her
mother happy…that would make *her* happy. She
wanted to be married to the father of her baby.

'Ha! As if that's likely,' she sniffed, tears burning
behind her eyes. She thought of all the times she'd

seen the man since the fateful night that had resulted in her present predicament, and not once had he said a word about the time they'd spent together. If she didn't have the absolute proof of it, she might almost think she'd imagined it.

As if she could have imagined anything that erotic. She might have a tendency to read steamy romances when she curled up in bed, but she'd been a virgin, for heaven's sake. A twenty-eight-year-old virgin who had been deliberately saving herself for the man she loved.

It had been completely accidental that he'd walked in on her and found her stark naked and dripping wet, drawn there by her shriek when the warm water she'd been anticipating had turned out to be icy cold.

The way his eyes had fixed on her naked breasts, widening and darkening as they'd reacted to his gaze, had been the first time she'd suspected that he had anything but platonic feelings for her—or had he just been taking advantage of circumstances?

Perhaps she'd never know unless she confronted him, and one day she was going to have to do just that, but in the meantime…

In the meantime she needed to get to sleep if she was going to be able to do her job in the morning. Tomorrow was going to be here all too soon.

'H'lo?'

Freya's mouth wasn't any wider awake than her brain, both dragged to life by the imperious command of the telephone.

'Freya? It's Finn. Are you awake?'

'No,' she muttered, her face still half-buried in the pillow as she longed for just a little more sleep. At least until her alarm woke her. These days she seemed to need far more than there were spare hours in the day.

Anyway, why was Finn phoning her at this time of night? What on earth would make him——?

'Mum!' she exclaimed, sitting bolt upright in bed, her head whirling from the sudden movement. 'Something's happened to Mum. What is it?' She hadn't felt this sick for weeks.

'Freya, no!' he interrupted, almost having to shout to make her listen. 'She's all right, or at least she was when I spoke to her last.'

'She's all right?' The relief left her positively shaky…and crabby. 'Then what are you doing, phoning me at this time of night? What on earth was so important that it couldn't wait until I got to work? My alarm hasn't even gone off yet.'

'That's why I'm phoning you,' he said, apparently patiently, but she could hear a definite chuckle in his voice. 'Have you looked at the time yet?'

Freya peered through the gloom, only remembering at the last moment that she'd forgotten to open the curtains the way she usually did before she went to sleep.

'It's morning!' she yelped. 'I must have forgotten to set it. I'm going to be late!'

'Not if I give you a lift,' he pointed out just as she was about to hang up. 'Buzz me in.'

Already frantically trying to remember whether she'd left clean clothes ready and whether she'd have time to grab something to eat, she didn't think twice about reaching for the button that would buzz through to unlock the electronic safety device on the front door.

Finn must have taken the stairs two at a time because he was knocking on her door before she'd even got as far as stepping under the shower.

'You could have waited in the car,' she pointed out with her ratty old chenille dressing-gown clutched around her and her dark curly hair sticking out from her head and hanging down her back like an electrocuted mop. 'There isn't even time for you to sit down if we're going to get there for the start of our shift.'

'Well, get moving, then, sunshine,' he ordered, pointing towards the sound of the running shower. 'You've got precisely two minutes.'

Freya whirled round with a muffled shriek. It would take that long just to get her dratted hair into some sort of order, let alone drying and dressing.

'I'm going to have this lot chopped off,' she growled as she emerged five minutes later, still struggling with a wide-toothed comb. There hadn't been enough time to dry herself properly so her clothes were sticking uncomfortably to her clammy body, but as for her hair...

'Don't you dare,' he threatened as he took the comb from her hand and replaced it with a slice of toast, thickly buttered and with a generous layer of her mother's home-made marmalade.

'I haven't got time to eat this,' she mumbled around her first delicious bite, deliberately squashing down her instant reaction to the intimacy of his task.

'You haven't got time *not* to eat it,' he disagreed ruthlessly, already beginning the time-consuming task of smoothing the long strands into some sort of order ready for Freya to tie them back out of the way. Untamed, they would coil themselves into a dark waterfall of uncontrollable natural spirals within minutes.

'You need to fuel the engine, especially in your condition,' Finn continued with a nudge towards the glass of milk he'd poured for her. 'Anyway, you're going to have to hit the ground running today if you're going to be taking time off while your mum's in hospital.'

'How did you know that's what I—? Oh, you spoke to her after I did last night? How did she sound?' Freya tried to turn towards him but he had too tight a hold on the last section of her hair.

'Stand still or I'm going to lose this comb for ever,' he warned. 'Actually, she phoned me and she's fine, especially since I hinted that you might have a surprise for her?'

'A surprise?' She groaned. 'A shock is more like it. Why did you have to do that? I'm still trying to come up with some way that she won't have to know—'

'I might have a solution,' he interrupted, this time unable to stop her whirling to face him. Luckily, she'd already half emptied the glass of milk in her hand or it might have gone all over him.

'You have? What?' she demanded impatiently, excitement and relief suddenly flooding through her.

'Here. Do something with this,' he directed far too calmly, handing her back the comb to finish the task of taming her hair then retrieving his own piece of toast and a banana for each of them.

'Finn!' she wailed while she dextrously wound the thick damp mass into a coil and secured it at the back of her head with a heavy-duty bronze clasp. 'Tell me!'

'No time,' he said with one hand on her back as he ushered her towards the door. 'We're due on duty in about three and a half minutes. And anyway,' he continued over his shoulder as he led the way down the stairs, leaving her no chance to argue, 'I've still got to make some enquiries to see if my solution is possible, and I'd rather not say anything till I've found out the answers.'

CHAPTER THREE

FINN had to navigate the usual early morning traffic while Freya spent the whole journey trying to change his mind, but he was adamant.

'Hopefully, I'll have some answers by the end of the day,' he offered as he parked the car in its designated spot close to the accident and emergency unit. He still couldn't believe that he'd even had the nerve to come up with the idea in the first place, let alone that he was going to try to persuade her to carry it out. That was, if he got the answers he needed.

'The end of the day?' she echoed in dismay. 'I was going to speak to Mum during my lunch-break and she's bound to want details. I'm not even going to know what I'm not supposed to be telling her if you don't give me a clue.'

'Tell her to "wait and see", the way she always tells you,' he said with a chuckle, knowing Freya definitely wouldn't appreciate it if he told her she looked like a little girl about to stamp a petulant foot. 'I've heard you say you'll get your revenge on her one day, and this could be the ideal chance.'

'It's only getting my revenge if *I* know what I'm keeping a secret,' she pointed out with a grumpy pout, and Finn was tempted to plant a swift kiss on it. That would give her something else to think about.

On the other hand...

No. Wrong time, wrong place, wrong fantasy.

'Look, there really isn't time for this now,' he said as he strode towards the main portico, completely disregarding the fact that her shorter legs meant she was almost running to keep up with him. 'If you don't want to risk inadvertently saying something misleading to her, you could always delay your call home until I've done my checking. Anyway,' he pointed out with a smug grin, 'it's your turn to feed me this time, so I'll give you a lift home.'

Freya spluttered a bit in his wake, but as her arrival in the unit coincided almost to the second with a warning about incoming ambulances from a gas explosion, he knew he was off the hook for the foreseeable future.

Freya was totally frustrated.

Finn had been hardly more than a few yards away from her all morning but she was no closer to being able to pin him down than if he'd moved to the opposite end of the hospital.

The explosion had been a bad one. By all accounts the cause had been a badly maintained boiler system in an old factory. As it had also brought down a main load-bearing wall and a section of the upper floor with it, the injuries they'd been treating had been out of all proportion to the size of the initial blast.

'This is almost like those old films you see of injuries during the two world wars,' one of the junior nurses had commented in horrified tones.

Freya looked at the mixture of burns, scalds, fractures, lacerations and other wounds surrounding them and couldn't help agreeing. Then she met Finn's eyes across the trauma room and knew that he, too, was remembering that there were wars and natural disasters going on around the world at any time, each producing just such a catalogue of injuries.

They both knew only too well that there was no need to go back half a century to look for the evidence. They'd both been there and seen it less than a year ago, shortly after she'd moved to St David's. They'd both been part of a group of volunteers trying to help out in a refugee camp after the latest flare-up in the seemingly never-ending conflicts around the edges of the former Soviet Union.

That journey had opened her eyes, taking her completely out of her own world and introducing her to a much harsher one. She and Finn had grown much closer in those grim days, talking for hours as they'd shared their experiences. She'd actually begun to think that they might one day...

Then had come that fateful conference and their torturous journey to get home in time to celebrate the twins' birthday, and her life had been changed for ever. And the saddest thing, for her, was that she hadn't been able to talk to Finn about it, in spite of the fact that they'd known each other for so long, in spite of...

'Freya?' Finn's call snapped her out of her fruitless introspection. Her hands and brain had apparently been continuing their task without needing her conscious supervision, but it looked as if he had a fight on his hands and needed her help.

'What's the problem?' Her eyes were already cataloguing the fact that the bulky man between them had a dislocated shoulder.

'Derek was apparently helping to rescue some of the people trapped by the explosion—'

'I was trying to get my girlfriend out,' Derek interrupted quickly. 'Can someone find out if she's safe yet?'

'She was trapped in the building, too?' Freya asked, immediately concerned over the unknown woman's safety, especially in view of the severity of some of the injuries they'd seen.

'She'd gone to the ladies just before it happened but nobody had seen her since. Can you ask if the firemen have got to her yet?'

'Do they know to look for her?' Finn demanded. 'They should have a list of all the employees on the premises so they can keep track.'

'I doubt that the bast— Sorry, Doctors,' he interrupted himself when the word slipped out. 'I doubt that the so-and-so's who run that place even know the names of the people, let alone have them written down. It's a right sweatshop but when people are desperate for work and don't want too many questions asked…'

'As soon as we've sorted you out we'll tell you who to speak to to get some up-to-date news,' Freya promised.

'In the meantime, we need to get on with this,' Finn continued. 'Derek slightly overestimated his strength and when the beam shifted…' He gestured silently towards the clear evidence of a dislocated shoulder. 'Anyway, I've told him that he needs this reducing before it does any permanent damage to his joint or the rest of his arm, but he doesn't want any pain relief.' Freya hoped she was the only one who could hear the frustrated edge to Finn's voice.

She'd never seen so many muscles on a man, outside a cartoon of a superhero. His arms were enormous, with muscles that were probably bigger than most people's legs. Without some means of pain relief it was highly unlikely that Finn would be able to get sufficient traction to reposition the ball joint in the socket.

Perhaps his refusal was an ego thing. Perhaps the man was under the impression that his bodybuilding friends would think he was a wimp for needing pain relief. If that's what it was, she needed to come up with a face-saving option.

She thought for a moment then leant a little closer to their stubborn patient. 'You don't have to worry about any pain relief we give you showing up on any dope tests,' she promised with a smile. 'By the time this shoulder's ready for competition again there's absolutely no possibility that there'll be any residue in your body. It's quick-acting, effective and easy for your body to get rid of.'

'That's not the problem,' he muttered, without meeting her eyes. 'I can't bear needles and I'm claustrophobic. That's why I got into bodybuilding in the first place—because I passed out when they gave me a needle at school for a vaccination and I got bullied.'

Finn stood there with one eyebrow raised, as though challenging her to find a solution. He'd obviously already tried to overcome the man's phobia by stressing the fact that the longer the arm remained misplaced the greater the chance that there might be permanent damage to the nerves and blood supply.

And all the time she was aware that there were many more patients waiting for the two of them.

'Do you ever stop to smell flowers?' she asked suddenly, and saw both men blink.

'Roses,' he muttered. 'My granddad used to grow them on his allotment and bring them to Gran on Sundays.'

'So, if I were to give you a flower to sniff, you wouldn't be afraid I was going to suffocate you?' she prompted, already exchanging the adult-sized mask on the gas-and-air line for a much smaller one.

She held the mask out to him and was glad when he took it, in spite of his clear reluctance.

'All you have to do is hold it up to your nose and breathe in a few times,' she said matter-of-factly. 'You're in total control of it. Neither of us will touch it.'

She held her breath for a moment while she deliberately smiled her encouragement, and was rewarded by a first tentative breath.

'If you can get in a couple of big ones, it will probably be enough to do the job,' Finn said with a smile. He had one hip resting on the edge of the bed with his arms folded across the width of his own considerable chest as though he had all the time in the world.

'Doesn't smell like Granddad's roses,' Derek muttered, but at least he was taking the deep breaths they needed to get the stuff into his system.

'Traction and distraction,' Finn murmured as he took up his position and explained carefully what he was going to do.

'Shall I wrap a draw sheet around his chest to apply opposing traction?' Freya offered, knowing that Finn was going to need all the help he could get with someone this muscular.

'No. Thank you,' Finn said, his voice sounding unexpectedly curt. Freya was startled until she saw the direction of his sharp gaze—towards her hidden pregnancy. The realisation that he didn't want her to do anything strenuous enough to endanger the baby sent a sharp spiral of happiness through her.

'Verbal distraction will have to do,' he added with a wry grin as he heeled off one shoe and placed his sock-clad foot high up on Derek's ribcage, almost into his armpit, while he took a firm hold on the affected arm.

'How's the level of pain?' Freya asked, but Derek was too busy taking another deep breath to answer.

'Try to relax,' Finn prompted, and Freya could see from the bulging in his muscles that, in spite of the relaxing effect of the Entonox, Derek was still tending to fight his efforts.

'So, Derek, what sort of training do you do to build up muscles like this?' she asked cheerfully. 'Have you got as far as bench-pressing buses yet, or do you limit it to small cars?'

That bit of nonsense obviously did the trick. It had distracted Derek just long enough for Finn to do the job. There was an audible snick as the ball and socket were reunited, then Finn burst out laughing.

'Bench-pressing buses?' he repeated, sharing a grin with his patient as he gently checked that there was no restriction to the arm's movement, then positioned it carefully across the man's chest ready to be strapped in a sling. 'I think he's graduated to Centurion tanks at least.'

Freya couldn't help grinning as she followed Finn out of the room, especially when she heard him muttering, 'Smell the flowers!'

'Just because *you* couldn't get him to comply,' she teased.

He opened his mouth to retaliate but someone was calling for him. They both heard the urgency and simultaneously whirled and started to hurry towards the emergency entrance.

'This is the last victim from the gas blast. We'd nearly given up on locating her then finally found her in a toilet,' the paramedic added.

'Derek's girlfriend!' Freya exclaimed, stepping forward eagerly.

'You already know more about her than we do.' The paramedic laughed. 'She was unconscious when we found her and hasn't surfaced at all on the way in.'

The nurses were already removing the remaining pieces of her damaged clothing and that was when Freya saw what Derek hadn't told them.

'She's pregnant.'

'And she's fractured her pelvis,' the paramedic added, suddenly all business. 'So far all her readings are fairly stable and within normal ranges, but she looks pretty close to term and she's got an enormous lump on the side of her head.'

Freya was listening as she began her own examination. She had her gloved hand resting against the side of the young woman's swollen belly when she felt an unwelcome tightening sensation in the underlying muscles.

'Gentlemen, the problem just got worse,' she announced. 'I think she's in labour.'

'Damn,' Finn muttered grimly. 'She can't go through that. Not in the state she's in. We'll have to do a Caesarean. Now.'

'Blood pressure's dropping,' called a voice somewhere behind them.'

'How fast?' Finn demanded.

'Too fast.' Freya was trying to keep an eye on everything at once while sterile packs were torn open, drips set up and the necessary drugs injected. A phone call meant that extra type-O blood was already on the way, and type-specific wouldn't be far behind as soon as their patient's group had been cross-matched.

Almost before she registered that Finn had donned a clean pair of gloves and a mask, he was making a decisive incision in the swabbed skin of the prominent mound. Then he had to wait impatiently while precious seconds ticked away, but the latest contraction was still tightening the muscles to iron.

'Ready?' he demanded with a quick glance across at her from those moss green eyes, and then he was carefully making a neat opening in the wall of the uterus.

There was an immediate flood of fluid mixed with

blood, and the proportion of blood was worryingly high.

'Baby's alive...and it's a girl,' he announced as he lifted the pathetic scrap out in one broad hand and held her out to Freya and the cloth she held ready, the umbilical cord still visibly pulsing as it tethered mother and offspring for those last precious seconds.

She paused only long enough for the cord to be cut then turned away to hand her frail burden to the waiting paediatrician.

By the time she turned back her place had already been taken by the orthopaedic surgeon who would be responsible for stabilising the shattered pelvis. Finn was still busy completing his part of the process, with the placenta to remove and the incision to repair, and all of them were aware that it needed to be done in the shortest possible time. Their patient's life depended on all of them finding and stopping every source of blood loss if they were to stem the woman's drop in blood pressure.

Freya would have liked to have stayed to watch, fascinated as ever by the skilful elegance of those long-fingered hands, but there were too many other people still patiently waiting for attention.

It was nearly an hour before she caught sight of Finn again and in that time she'd had ample cause to be very relieved that this wasn't her first encounter with such a number and variety of injuries.

Her latest patient wasn't nearly so serious but was causing almost more of a problem than any of them.

'Adrienne, let the doctor have a look at your head, darling,' coaxed the flustered mother. 'I promise she won't hurt you.'

Her screaming daughter wasn't having it, in spite of the fact that the back of her long blonde hair was liberally streaked with blood.

'No!' she shrieked as she buried her face in her mother's neck. 'Don't want doctor. Want to go home to party!'

'Having problems?' Finn asked, his deep voice only just audible beneath the barrage of sound.

Freya sighed. 'She's supposed to be having a birthday party.'

'Did one of the guests mug her for her presents?' he muttered, and Freya was hard put to keep the grin off her face.

'Apparently, she got a little over-excited and was bouncing on her brothers' bunk bed.'

'And cracked the back of her head when she fell off,' he finished in a tone that said he'd heard the story all too often before. 'Have you managed to make any sort of examination yet?'

'What do you think?' she challenged wryly. 'She took one look at me in my gloves and that was it.'

'So what you need is some sort of serious diversion so you can see what you're dealing with.'

'And some serious prayers that she doesn't need to

be kept in overnight,' she added. 'I don't think any-one in the whole hospital would get any sleep tonight if she had to miss her birthday party.'

'Give me a few minutes to come up with something and then be prepared to move quickly. You might need sutures if it's a particularly bad gash, but more often than not you'll be able to get by if you can glue it.'

'What are you going to…?' He was gone before she could finish the question, leaving her with the noisy four-year-old and an increasingly embarrassed mother.

'How old are your sons?' Freya asked the poor woman over the sound of her daughter's continuing howls, hoping an ordinary conversation might calm both of them down.

'Eight and six,' she replied distractedly.

'Are they waiting outside?'

'No. I've left them at home with my neighbour. The rest of Adrienne's playgroup are due to arrive soon, so there had to be someone there to explain what's happened.'

'How many are due?'

'Fifteen,' she said with a grimace. 'Boys and girls aged from three to five. I don't know how my poor neighbour is going to cope with them.'

'Won't their parents stay to supervise?' Freya could just imagine how much mischief that many preschoolers could get up to with only one supervisor. And she'd been wondering if she could cope with one…

'I don't know whether that would make it worse or better,' she admitted, the level of her voice nearly normal now that the volume of her daughter's distress was diminishing. Perhaps the lack of notice was helping the youngster to forget the reason she was there. 'It's only a small house. I can't imagine how that many children are going to fit in it, let alone their parents as well.'

'What on earth made you invite so many, then?' Would she remember this conversation when it was her own turn to arrange a birthday party?

'How do you invite some children from the group and leave out others without breaking their hearts?'

'Good point,' Freya conceded, wondering if she would one day have the same dilemma.

'Excuse me,' said a deep voice behind her, and Freya turned to see a handful of bright balloons protruding between the cubicle curtains. They were clutched by a lean male hand that she recognised only too well, but apart from a pair of well-polished black shoes, that was all she could see for the moment.

'Can you help me, please?' continued the voice. 'I'm looking for Adrienne, the birthday girl.'

'Adrienne, that's you!' her mother prompted, but there was no need. The child had obviously heard him and was already staring in disbelief at the enticing display.

'Who's that?' she whispered.

'Me!' Finn announced, poking just his head through the curtains so that it was framed by the balloons.

He had a huge red smiley mouth painted on his face and Freya wouldn't have had a clue who it was if she hadn't recognised his voice.

'I'm Bobo,' he announced with a quick wink in Freya's direction that told her to move as fast as she could. 'And I'm bringing big bright beautiful balloons for a big brave beautiful birthday princess. Do you want to see them?'

He came into the cubicle and crouched down beside the bemused youngster, keeping up a stream of chatter that had her so captivated that she barely noticed when Freya enlisted her mother's help to hold her long hair out of the way. There was no complaint at all once the gash was sprayed with a local anaesthetic then quickly cleaned before the edges were neatly aligned for gluing together.

In spite of the fact that she was concentrating on completing her task, she hadn't missed the game Finn had played with his torch, or the thumbs-up he'd given her, telling her that their little patient's eyes were reacting normally to the light.

'So, princess, are you ready to go home to your party?' Bobo asked when Freya indicated that she'd finished.

'I can't,' she said with a sudden wobble of her

lower lip. 'Jamie said I got to have a *noperation* on my head.'

'Well, princess, Bobo says the *noperation* is all over and it's time to go home and see if all your friends have arrived.'

Freya reminded her bemused mother to call at the registration desk for a copy of the advice sheet listing the common 'things to look out for' after a head injury and then there were just the two of them in the cubicle, herself and Bobo.

'I hope that isn't a kiss-proof lipstick,' she said with a sudden giggle, trying to imagine the poor man walking around all day with a big red smile painted on his face.

'Do you want to try it out?' he offered with a wicked twinkle and though she backed rapidly out of range, she couldn't help but admit that she'd been very tempted. It seemed such a long time since she'd been kissed. Four and a half months, to be precise.

'Spoilsport,' he teased. 'Shame it's only face paint left over from last summer's fundraiser.'

Freya tried to pretend that his antics were beneath her, but inside she couldn't help revelling in this playful side of the man.

When the occasion merited it Finn could be every bit the stern professional man, and she didn't have to look very far to find any number of women who admired the fact that he was big and gorgeous and sexy.

At their family get-togethers he was everything that

a loving brother and uncle should be, and his rapport with his patients was well known, as was his sense of fun.

Was she the only one who had a sneaking suspicion that, deep down, the man who apparently had it all wasn't truly happy?

She didn't have anything concrete on which to base her conviction, but ever since the day she'd met him—that same fateful day when she'd watched her sister fall madly in love with his brother—she'd had the feeling that he was hiding something. What it was…an inadmissible secret, hidden emotion, impossible dream…she had no idea, but for some time she'd wondered if that was the reason why he'd tried to keep her at arm's length for so long.

Was that the reason why he never allowed their private conversations to stray towards anything that could be construed as personal? Was that why he'd never even mentioned that single time when they'd…

'By the way,' he added as he set off towards the cloakroom to get rid of his over-decorated face, 'I've been promised some answers to my potential solution by five o'clock this afternoon. I'll give you a lift home from work and tell you the results.'

Freya had to stifle a growl of frustration. She never liked being strung along and he knew it. Even as a child she'd hated seeing those fascinating parcels piling up under the tree, knowing that she wasn't allowed to touch until Christmas Day. She'd preferred not to know anything about them till the appointed day than be taunted with their presence.

Finn knew exactly what it was going to do to her to know that he had set something in motion. She knew him well enough to know that she wouldn't get anything out of him until he was ready, but why did he have to tell her about the prospect, knowing she was going to be seething with anticipation until then?

Thank goodness she'd learned to subdue most of her emotions while she had patients to tend, she thought after a self-indulgent couple of minutes spent dreaming up suitable vengeance against Finn for leaving her in limbo.

For all her practice at keeping herself slightly detached from the horrors she saw on a daily basis, there was no way that she could deal unemotionally with her final patient of the shift. It struck far too close to home for that.

'Please, please, please,' the woman was panting softly, almost as if it were some sort of mantra. Her eyes were tightly closed, as though to shut out a prospect too dreadful to face, and her hands were curved rigidly across her abdomen.

'Please, Doctor,' said the grey-faced man who accompanied her into the room. 'Save our baby. We only found out about it a few days ago and now she's in agony and she's bleeding.'

It took every bit of Freya's skill to drag out of him the fact that after five years of marriage they'd finally given up trying for a baby at Christmas, using the money they'd saved for a final round of in-vitro fertilisation to have a much-needed holiday in the sun.

'She only went to the doctor because her periods hadn't returned after the last course of treatment and…and there it was on the scan.'

Freya could hear the echo of their ecstatic surprise in his voice and suddenly realised that their baby must have been conceived at almost the same time as hers.

The sudden shock as she tried to imagine how she would be feeling at this moment if it had been *her* lying on that bed left her brain frozen.

'Freya?'

That was Finn's voice, and his hand on her arm turning her away from the tear-stained woman to face him.

'I'll deal with this one,' he said gruffly, his warm hands bracketing both her elbows in an infinitely supportive grip. 'Go and get yourself a cup of tea before you keel over.'

She looked up into those green eyes and could have drowned in the ocean of concern she saw there.

Instead, she stiffened her spine.

'I'm all right,' she insisted. 'I just need to—'

'You just need to do as you're told,' he interrupted firmly.

Surprise left her with her mouth hanging open for several seconds.

'You're pulling rank?' she demanded, barely remembering to keep her voice down. 'While I'm in the middle of dealing with a patient?'

'If that's how you want to see it,' he agreed smoothly. 'Either way, I'm taking over because you're now officially off duty.'

He gently used his grip on her arms to turn her around to face the door then calmly faced the distraught couple and introduced himself.

The whole scene had happened so quickly that luckily no one else in the room seemed to have noticed anything going on. But Freya knew, and as she stalked indignantly out into the corridor she felt as if, instead of a fellow professional, she'd been treated like a child—metaphorically patted on the head and sent away to play somewhere else.

And it wasn't even as if she could go home to nurse her hurt feelings, she seethed as she made for the nearest kettle. She'd already agreed to wait for the wretched man so he could tell her what he'd spent the day planning, or investigating, or plotting, or whatever else he was up to.

'And wouldn't you just know it!' she exclaimed in disgust. 'There are no teabags left.' And she'd been religiously avoiding coffee ever since she'd first realised that she was pregnant. The baby might not have been planned, but she was certainly going to look after it every bit as well as if it had been.

She slumped down into the chair closest to the bank of windows and stared blankly out at the shadows. They were starting to lengthen under the group of young trees that formed part of the landscaping that had taken place when this wing had been added several years ago.

Sweet chestnuts, she registered in some vague corner of her mind. The branches were covered in the typical pyramids of flowers that would produce edible nuts in the autumn. Two trees had creamy white flowers while the third had more than a hint of raspberry pink about it.

There had been one like it at the bottom of the garden when she was growing up, she remembered with a soft smile. Every year she and Astrid had gone with their mother to collect a small sack of nuts from the prickly seed cases so that there would be some ready for chestnut stuffing for the Christmas turkey.

Suddenly, the enormity of everything that was going on in her life overwhelmed her and she buried her face in her hands, barely managing to stop the tears from falling.

She didn't know if her mother had continued to make that little pilgrimage once she and Astrid had left home, or whether it had been something she'd done especially with them. Would her mother even be alive this Christmas when it was time to make the chestnut stuffing?

She desperately needed to go home to see her, to wrap her arms around her and breathe in the familiar scent of her favourite lavender, just in case she never had another chance.

But she didn't dare.

Until…*unless* Finn had managed to come up with some foolproof method of keeping the fact of her pregnancy from her mother, Freya didn't dare risk what the shock of discovery might do to her damaged heart.

She unearthed a crumpled tissue and mopped up as best she could, grateful that she didn't have to worry about streaky make-up. She'd always been grateful for the thick, dark eyelashes that didn't need any artifice, much to her much blonder sister's chagrin.

For just a moment she contemplated ringing Astrid, but then remembered that she was probably just as bad as their mother at picking up on her moods. She certainly wouldn't be able to get away with saying that there was nothing wrong when the topic she desperately wanted to talk about was the one she mustn't mention.

She leant her head wearily against the glass and forced herself to think about her patients instead.

Had Finn been able to do anything for that poor woman or had she lost her precious baby? And how about the woman who had been pulled out of the gas explosion? Had she regained consciousness yet? Had the staff been able to tell her that her baby was holding her own out in the big wide world?

She straightened up again when she realised that

thinking about patients wasn't working either. Every time she came back to the same topic…babies. It was just too hard to switch her brain away from the topic now that her pregnancy was the one thing standing between her and her overwhelming need to see her mother with her own eyes.

Where was Finn, for heaven's sake?

Freya realised that it had only been a matter of hours since she'd told him why she hadn't been home for months. Surely he understood that she'd been turning herself inside out for months now, wanting to find a way to break the news of her impending motherhood to her family. Didn't he realise that she was going to be a gibbering wreck if he dragged this out any longer? And if it was her fault that anything happened to her mother…

CHAPTER FOUR

SHE looked so sad…almost defeated, Finn thought as he paused silently in the doorway. And that just didn't seem right for Freya.

The woman he knew—*hell*, the woman he'd been having erotic dreams about almost since the first time he'd met her—wasn't one to let life get her down. It had taken something of this magnitude to put a dent in her impregnable armour and he felt an answering ache.

More than an ache, in fact. If he ever found out the name of the man who'd made her pregnant and then left her to face the consequences alone, well, if he had his way, the guy would never be in a position to do it again.

And that had nothing to do with the fact that he was almost green with jealousy, that he'd wanted Freya for more than six years with a single-minded possessiveness that he'd never felt towards a woman before.

He hadn't wanted it to happen—at twenty-eight he certainly wouldn't have fallen for an innocent twenty-one-year-old if he'd had a choice. And what man would be happy with the idea that the woman he wanted for himself had come into his life on his brother's arm? What was worse, she hadn't so much as looked at another man since Colum had fallen for Astrid.

How many times had he cursed the length of time it was taking her to get over him? Now all he could do was wish it had taken just a little bit longer—just long enough for him to realise that she was ready to start dating again and might just see him as a willing replacement for her lost love.

He felt almost guilty when he thought about the way he was going to try to take advantage of the present situation, but when this second chance had landed right in front of him he'd known that he couldn't afford to let it go. Not if he was going to remain sane.

Now all he had to do was try to persuade her that his wild scheme would serve her purpose in the short term. Then, with time on his side, he would have to use every strategy he possessed to persuade her to make it permanent.

'Finn?'

He must have moved or made a sound because suddenly Freya was up out of her chair and hurrying towards him.

'What happened? She didn't lose the baby, did she?' Those wide grey eyes were searching his face for clues, already full of sympathetic tears.

'Baby's safe so far,' he reassured her, and she

blessed him with one of those smiles that always made it feel as if the sun had come out. 'The pain and the blood in her urine were due to a simple kidney infection so we've put her on antibiotics. The scan showed no signs of any problems with the baby.'

'Oh, thank God,' she breathed, clearly almost as pleased as if it were her own child she was talking about. 'I was so worried for them. After giving up on the IVF and then conceiving naturally…the chances of that happening again were…' She shook her head wordlessly, but he didn't need her to say anything more. They both knew that if the couple lost this child they would probably be losing their last chance of having the baby they'd tried so desperately to conceive.

'And if you want some more good news,' he added, determined not to give in to the temptation to touch her, to hold her, 'the patient rescued from the toilet after the gas explosion? Derek-the-bodybuilder's girlfriend? She woke up about an hour ago.'

'Really? How is she?' Freya's delight was unfeigned, but that was just one of the things he admired about her—the fact that she was interested in her patients as people, that she really cared about them.

'Honestly?' He grimaced when he thought about the number and complexity of the injuries that had become evident once they had a complete set of X-rays. 'She's a mess. Her pelvis is a giant three-dimensional jigsaw that's going to have to be held together with wire, plates and screws while it mends. It'll probably be months before she even stands up, let alone tries to walk.'

'But she'll recover?' It was definitely more of a statement than a question. 'And she'll have her baby, too. When will she be able to see her?'

'Freya, we work in Accident and Emergency,' he reminded her patiently. 'What happens to our patients once we hand them over to other departments is out of our remit.'

'Yes. I know. But surely *someone* will make sure she gets to see her baby. Soon.'

'Persistent little thing, aren't you?' he grumbled. 'Well, just to get you off everyone's back, Derek is running relays between the two of them and he's arguing just as hard as you are to get the two of them together. And remembering the size of him, I don't think it'll be long before it happens.'

Freya chuckled and her wide grey eyes sparkled with shared mirth. 'No. I can't imagine anyone standing in his way for long, even with one hand tied down.'

For a moment Finn was trapped in those silvery gleams and the tendrils of a hundred dreams wrapped themselves around him. Her eyes shining up at him in the muted glow of some unknown room, filled with a mixture of shyness and bravado as she stood before him wearing nothing but rivulets of water.

How many times had he woken up convinced that

he'd spent the night running his fingers through the long silky spirals of her dark hair, draping them over her shoulders and across her breasts before he became distracted by her silky skin and the tight rosy crests of her nipples. Waking up so aroused that—

'Finn?'

Her voice was as uncertain as the expression on her face and he cursed silently, wondering just how much of his thoughts had been displayed in his eyes.

It wasn't the first time her laughter had turned him on and it probably wouldn't be the last. In fact, if she accepted the suggestion he was going to put to her tonight, he was probably condemning himself to months of utter hell, because it wasn't just her laughter that affected him. Just being in the same room was enough to—

'Finn? Is everything all right?' she demanded. 'Your mind's obviously somewhere else. If you've got something you'd rather be doing tonight...'

'No, Freya, nothing,' he said firmly. 'This situation with your mother is important and you need to get it sorted out as soon as possible for her sake. She needs to be concentrating on her own health, not worrying about you.'

'If you're sure...' she began again, and he allowed himself the luxury of taking her by the arm.

'Come on, woman. Time to leave this place and get to more important things...like food,' he teased. 'Remember, you're supposed to be feeding me.'

They had to pass a take-away pizza place on the way to her flat and he made sure to groan when she insisted that she couldn't live another moment without at least one slice laden with spicy sausage and extra cheese.

He would have preferred the distraction of preparing a meal but he had to admit that it would only be postponing the inevitable. Either she would grab at his solution or she'd laugh in his face, and as far as he could tell nothing he could do would influence her reaction either way.

They'd barely stepped inside the flat when the phone rang.

Freya had automatically stepped out of her shoes as soon as she was inside the door and was padding barefoot into the tiny kitchen area with her nose hanging greedily over the boxed pizza, so Finn was closer and automatically lifted the receiver.

'Freya's residence. This is the butler speaking,' he quipped, grinning at the face she pulled at him while she grabbed a handful of paper towels ready to wipe greasy fingers after they'd eaten.

'Finn! I'm glad you're there,' said a familiar voice and he felt the smile fade. Freya's father was a very level-headed man and he could think of only one reason why the man should sound quite so strung up.

'Is everything all right?' he demanded quietly, hoping that Freya wouldn't realise who was on the other end until he knew the extent of the problem. The fact that he felt so protective of her was something he would have to think about another time.

'Yes and no,' Stuart Innes said. 'There's been a cancellation on the surgeon's list so they want Ruth to go in early. The surgery would be in just over two weeks' time, which is fantastic. The stubborn woman's refusing even to think about it until she's seen Freya.'

'When do they want her to go in?' Finn's mind was working at warp speed. He'd been counting on the leeway of the next couple of days to persuade Freya to accept his solution. Perhaps this way would be better—give her too little time to think about it and realise how crazy it was.

As it was, she'd realised who was on the other end of the line and was now hovering at his elbow, trying to hear her father's side of the conversation to find out what was happening. Thank goodness for the good manners that prevented her from snatching the receiver out of his hand.

'She's supposed to go into the General late on the Tuesday morning so they can do all the usual work-ups. The surgery slot is early Wednesday afternoon, all being well.'

'How soon do you have to let them know one way or the other?'

'An hour ago,' he said with a groan. 'If Peter Donaldson weren't a personal friend we'd have lost it already. Thank goodness he knows what Ruth's like when she gets a bee in her bonnet.'

'It'll take me ten minutes or so to get back to you…twenty at the outside,' Finn promised, then put the phone down without giving Freya a chance to speak.

The churning sensation inside him was making him glad he hadn't eaten anything yet and one glance at Freya's eyes was enough to tell him that this was going to be a fraught conversation. She was already wound up as tightly as a high-tensile steel spring and was now royally ticked off that he'd monopolised an important conversation with her father.

'So?' she demanded with an angry flush accentuating the soft curve of her cheeks. 'Are you going to tell me why *my* father rang me up on *my* phone? If I find out it's something about Mum and you didn't let me speak to—'

'They want her to go into hospital in two weeks,' he announced bluntly, then bitterly regretted it when she went as white as a sheet. She didn't even seem to notice that he was almost carrying her over to the settee.

'She's suddenly got worse?' she gasped, and her teeth were chattering like castanets as she forced the words out. 'Is it my fault? It *is*, isn't it? It's because she's been worrying about me.'

'No, Freya. It's nothing like that.' He closed his eyes in a mixture of pleasure and pain as he wrapped a comforting arm around her and cradled her against his side. She seemed so fragile in her distress and so infinitely precious. 'Purely and simply, the hospital had a cancellation and Peter Donaldson offered her the earlier spot.'

'You're sure? Oh, thank God that's all it is,' she groaned. 'I was afraid she'd collapsed or something.'

He heard the shuddering breath she released and felt her wilt against his side with the release of tension.

He certainly didn't feel the same way. If anything his tension was greater now that she was curled willingly against him. How was he supposed to make his brain work logically when he was breathing in the last lingering scent of the shampoo she'd used this morning? The delicate flowery smell of it seemed to have been following him all day since he'd combed the tangles out.

He hated to destroy the small calm oasis surrounding them, but he knew that her father was waiting for him to call and the sooner he broke the rest of the news to her the sooner he could pose his solution.

'The trouble is, your mother's still refusing to go into hospital until she's seen you,' he said quietly. 'She won't even accept the cancellation.'

'Damn,' she said with a wealth of feeling, and struggled to her feet, apparently oblivious to the fact that Finn hadn't wanted to release her. 'I was actually hoping that it would have the opposite effect—that her mind would be taken up so much with the fact that the operation had been brought forward that she'd completely forget about a visit from me. What am I going to do now?'

Her final words emerged more like a wail and he took a brief second to register the unusual sight of Freya Innes coming unravelled.

Since he'd first met her six years ago he'd seen her in every sort of mood, from doting and playful with her nephews to efficiently professional when she was working. He'd never seen her this close to losing control before and could only hope that it would give him the edge in the next few minutes. At the very least he needed to be on his feet in case what he suggested was too much of a shock for her.

'I've got a suggestion, if you'd like to think about it,' he offered, hoping his voice sounded calmer than he felt. Her mother's imminent heart surgery, set against the inevitable revelation of Freya's pregnancy, was potentially explosive. It was obvious that Freya must have been turning herself inside out over the last few months as she'd tried to find a way to break the news, knowing how it would disappoint Ruth.

The fact that he hoped he had found a way to keep both of them from going into self-destruct mode, while at the same time fulfilling one of his own dearest wishes, was probably too good to be true. Still, he thought as he took a calming breath and surreptitiously crossed his fingers for luck, he would never know if it was going to work if he didn't try.

'If you've found a way to turn back the clock or, better yet, turn it forward to when the operation's all over and I can visit her, knowing I'm not going to put her life in danger…' Freya quipped, but he could see the threat of tears in her over-bright grey eyes in spite of the subdued lighting.

'I'm still working on my time-travel machine, but in the meantime, instead of giving her the chance to grill you on why you haven't visited in the last couple of months, why not give her something else to get her teeth into.'

'Like what?' she demanded as the hopeful expression she'd worn for just a few moments began to fade. 'There isn't time to win a Nobel Peace Prize in two weeks, and winning a million on the lottery is unlikely as I don't even buy tickets, but it would take something of that magnitude to divert the inquisition.'

'How about a wedding?' he suggested, wondering if she could hear the way that his heart was suddenly trying to pound its way out of his chest. When had the outcome of any conversation meant so much to him?

'A wedding? What are you talking about?' she demanded, a frown pleating the pale skin between dark, sleek eyebrows. 'What has going to someone's wedding got to do with Mum's operation?'

'Not *someone's* wedding,' he corrected, feeling the

heat in his cheeks that told him he must rapidly be turning the colour of a ripe tomato. What on earth had given him this crazy idea in the first place, let alone persuaded him that he could sell it to her? Still, he couldn't go back now. He'd already leapt off the board and there was just time to take a deep breath before he found out whether he was going to sink or swim. 'How about ours?'

'Ours?' she parroted. 'Our what?'

He nearly groaned aloud. Where was her quick wit when he needed it? Was she going to make him spell everything out in words of one syllable?

'Our wedding,' he said, and when he saw the shock widening her eyes he hurried into the brief explanation he'd been trying to rehearse at intervals all day. 'Think about it,' he urged, forestalling the instant denial he was sure he saw forming on her lips. 'It would solve all your problems in one go. Your mother would be so bowled over by the surprise of it that she wouldn't have time to rake you over the coals. And by the time she *does* realise you're pregnant, her major objection won't exist any more so she won't be nearly so upset that you haven't stuck to the letter of her teaching.'

For several seconds Freya was completely speechless, just long enough for him to wonder just how much more of a shock it would have been if he'd added his own reason for making the offer. The trouble was, he couldn't be sure that his uninvited feelings for her might be the one thing to put her off the whole idea.

'Finn, you can't be serious,' she finally managed on an uneasy giggle.

'Oh, but I am. Perfectly serious,' he said steadily, able to meet her gaze unflinchingly because it was the complete truth. He'd been serious about this woman from the first time he'd met her and that hadn't changed in spite of the years that had passed.

He'd dated in that time, of course, but it had taken several years for him to realise that every petite, dark-haired woman had borne more than a passing similarity to Freya. Even when he'd consciously made himself spend time with tall blonde companions, it hadn't made a blind bit of difference. None of them were an acceptable substitute for the woman he wanted. And that was in spite of the fact that he knew he wasn't the man *she* wanted.

'But you *must* be joking,' she insisted. 'My mother is supposed to be going into hospital in two weeks and you're talking about announcing a wedding. That's not going to change anything as far as she's concerned.'

'It would if the wedding takes place in two weeks.'

'*Two weeks?*' she squeaked. 'Now I *know* you're joking. The stress of trying to organise a wedding in two weeks would kill her off completely. There's no way that anyone could get a wedding organised that fast.'

'Want to bet?' he said, and threw her a challenging grin as he reached for his wallet with one hand and the phone with the other.

It only took a moment to be connected to the hospital chaplain he'd contacted when the idea had first come to him, and a brief explanation of the change in the date of Ruth's operation was enough to alert the helpful man to the change of plan.

All the while Finn was confirming the arrangements he was watching the expressions chasing each other across Freya's face. They went from mockery to disbelief to utter amazement when he finally put the phone down and symbolically dusted his hands off.

'There you are,' he announced breezily, hoping she was buying his easy air when inside he was wound up tighter than a cheap watch. All it would take was a single word and the whole shaky edifice he'd been building would come tumbling down. 'One wedding all arranged without your mother knowing anything about it. All we have to do is give notice at the registry office tomorrow morning, then in fifteen days we put on a bit of spit and polish and pick up a bunch of flowers and we can get married.'

'Wh-what?' she gasped breathlessly, before exploding into speech. 'You're not serious, Finn! You couldn't possibly have organised everything with just one phone call. Who would be performing the ceremony? And where, for heaven's sake? It's impossible!'

'You're wrong, Freya. It's perfectly possible,' he said gently, and captured one of her flailing hands in his to lead her to her tiny two-seater settee before he continued.

'Once I knew the reason, I realised just how much it was hurting you to stay away from your family. I also know that your mother is definitely stubborn enough to refuse the surgery until you *have* been to see her. No matter how bad it could be for her health.'

'But...'

He pressed a finger to her lips to silence her, knowing he needed to get it all out before her proximity completely scrambled his brains.

'So,' he continued, 'I made a few enquiries and a few more phone calls so I knew it was all possible before I spoke to you.'

'That's why you wouldn't say anything earlier on today,' she commented, and the way her lips moved against his fingertip was a definite distraction.

'Exactly,' he said as he retrieved his hand and placed it out of temptation's way on his thigh, then used it to tick off her questions. 'First, as far as the legalities are concerned, we both need to go to present proof of our identities to the registrar when we go to give notice. After that, it's just a matter of waiting fifteen days. Second, two weeks should be plenty of time to buy something to wear and organise some flowers. If we were pushed, we could probably find a suitable bouquet in that little boutique in the main reception area of the General.

'Oh, and third, the man I was just talking to is the hospital chaplain and he's only too willing to perform the ceremony for us. Apparently, he doesn't have the chance to do it nearly as often as he'd like. As for work, I've spent part of today calling in a few favours for colleagues to cover for us. I've arranged for us to be off together for three days, starting on the Tuesday your mother goes in. Then, depending on your mother's progress, you've got the option for some extra leave on compassionate grounds.'

She was silent for such a long time after he'd finished speaking that he was certain that he'd completely blown it. He just knew that he'd gone too far with making all the arrangements when it was obvious that she was going to turn the whole crazy plan down.

Well, he'd known that thinking the solution to her problems was a last-minute marriage to keep her mother off the scent had been totally outrageous from the start. All he could do now was hope that he hadn't spoiled the informal friendship they'd built up over the last six years. If that was all they could have…

'Finn…why would you be willing to do such a thing?' she asked in a hesitant voice, her expression totally unreadable for a change and her words coming out in a disjointed fashion as if she was almost thinking aloud.

'The suggestion of marriage, I mean. It's such a serious step…such an extreme solution to come up with when you've hardly…when there's been nothing more than… It's not just some charitable thing, is it? You're not just saying it because you feel you ought to make the offer?'

'It's not charity,' he said hastily, suddenly frightened by the nuances suggested by her broken sentences. If she thought that the only reason he would offer to marry her was charity, the bastard who'd made her pregnant must have hurt her badly. The possibilities they conjured up weren't something he wanted to think about just at that moment.

'Look, I'm almost as concerned as you are about your mother's heart,' he agreed, 'but I wouldn't have offered marriage if I didn't think we stood some sort of chance of making a go of it. I wouldn't dare, knowing she's almost as vehemently against divorce as she is against illegitimacy.'

That teased a smile out of her, as he'd intended, but the frown was back far too soon.

'Finn,' she began, then huffed out an exasperated breath. 'You know as well as I do that the whole idea is completely, totally mad, but do you *really* think it could work?'

'If we're talking about easing your mother's mind so she'll go ahead with the operation then, yes, I think it'll work,' he said honestly. 'It'll be something so completely out of left field that she won't have time to think, let alone question, until the operation's all over and done with.'

'And the marriage?' she asked quietly, pinning him down just as he'd known she would, eventually.

'That's up to the two of us,' he said equally quietly, meeting her worried grey gaze with what he hoped was unwavering certainty in his own. 'Any marriage is only as strong as the amount of effort each of the partners is willing to put into it.'

He was sure that she had more questions but he almost breathed a sigh of relief when the phone rang again.

'That's probably your father, wanting to know if I've managed to persuade you to go home for a visit,' he reminded her, taking a step towards the instrument.

Suddenly, he gave in to an unexpected impulse and whirled back to sink to one knee in front of her, taking her hand in his and looking into her startled face. 'So, Freya, what's it going to be? Am I going to be the solution to the emergency? Your emergency groom?'

Finn wasn't absolutely certain whether he remembered to breathe while he waited for her reply. He knew it seemed to take aeons, although measured by the ringing of the telephone it must have only been seconds.

Seconds or aeons, it was long enough for him to

have time to be certain that he truly cared for this woman, cared enough to take her on in spite of the fact they'd never spoken words of love. He was also certain enough that he had plenty of love in his heart for Freya and for the child she carried, no matter who its father had been.

'All right,' she whispered, and for a moment he wasn't certain he'd heard her right.

'Was that a yes?' he demanded through a tight throat, hardly able to believe that six years of yearning might be coming to an end. 'You'll marry me?'

'Yes, Finn,' she said, smiling through a watery chuckle. 'I wouldn't want to waste all those careful arrangements you've made so, yes, I'll marry you.'

He hoped she couldn't see that his hand was trembling visibly as he reached for the phone, but there was nothing he could do to control it. He was tempted to give a rebel yell and was so full of churning emotions that he desperately wanted to talk to someone…wanted to tell them that Freya had actually accepted his…

'Finn? Stuart Innes here,' said the voice in his ear, and he knew that, for Freya's sake, he had to keep the lid on his exuberant feelings just a little while longer. 'Have you managed to talk some sense into that daughter of mine yet? Is she on her way? What time can I tell Ruth she'll be here?'

'You'll have to tell her mother she's going to have to compromise,' Finn warned the older man, suddenly realising with a shock of pleasure that he was talking to his future father-in-law. It was nice to know that he was finally going to be marrying into the family he already knew and genuinely liked. 'I'll be bringing Freya down myself, so you can go ahead and confirm Ruth's place on the surgeon's list. The problem is, we're heavily committed here so we won't be able to get to you until the day she's due to go into the General. You do have my solemn promise that we'll both come straight to the hospital.'

'Hmm. I don't know whether Ruth's going to go for that,' Stuart said dubiously. 'She said she wasn't going to budge from her own home until she'd seen Freya. Wretched woman.'

'I don't know whether you're talking about your wife or your daughter now,' he teased, and was glared at for his pains. 'Anyway, I'll leave it to you to work on the woman at your end of the phone. You can tell her that I promise I'll make the compromise well worth her while.'

'Oh?'

Finn knew he'd piqued the man's curiosity, and he was hoping that mysterious tone would do the same for Ruth.

It was such an overwhelming temptation to give them a hint. He still couldn't really believe that Freya had agreed, or that she would really go through with it. Was he secretly hoping that giving her parents a clue would be the insurance that would guarantee that Freya wouldn't back out at the last minute?

'All will be revealed when we arrive at the General,' he promised, surreptitiously crossing his fingers. Then, on a sudden inspiration he asked, 'I expect Astrid will be hovering while her mother's having all her tests?' Remembering Freya's role as bridesmaid at her sister's wedding, he was certain that Freya would want Astrid to be there for her own. That was a headache he still had to solve—how to get enough of both sides of the family there so that Freya didn't feel too badly short-changed.

'I expect both she and Colum will be there if they can find someone brave enough to take on those two hellion grandsons of mine,' Stuart said with a fond chuckle. 'Although I've had to threaten Astrid that she'll be banished until it's all over if she keeps crying. She'll only upset her mother if she carries on like that.'

'We'll definitely have to see if we can think of something to distract everybody,' Finn said. He grinned when he saw the way Freya rolled her eyes at him, but now that she'd actually agreed to the marriage he was really beginning to enjoy himself. For six years he'd carried the secret of his feelings towards this dark-haired sprite. This surprise wouldn't be nearly such a burden, especially as it would be revealed within a matter of days rather than years.

What would happen after that remained to be seen, but if he had his way…

CHAPTER FIVE

FREYA tugged the hem of her cream slubbed-silk jacket with shaky hands and drew in an equally shaky breath.

'Are you sure about this, Finn?' she whispered, hardly daring to look at him.

The first glimpse of him standing in the gloomy hallway outside her little flat had nearly made her swallow her tongue. To risk a clearer look at him in the clinical brightness of a hospital corridor was courting certain disaster. He was unfairly good-looking even in rumpled green scrubs at the end of a busy shift. In a tailor-made three-piece suit he was totally irresistible, even to a pregnant woman who was certain she was about to make one of the biggest mistakes of her life.

'Hey, Freya, calm down,' he murmured, catching hold of her elbow and drawing her to one side of the corridor. 'There's absolutely nothing to worry about. Everything's going to go like a dream and when it's all over you're going to wonder what all the fuss was about.'

'Can I have that in writing?' she muttered grimly. 'I've known my mother for twenty-nine years and

I've never managed to pull the wool over her eyes yet. I don't know what on earth made me think that this time would be any different.'

'Trust me,' he said persuasively, just a hint of that familiar wicked twinkle lightening those moss green eyes and sending an unexpected shiver of awareness skating up her spine. 'This time will be the exception that proves the rule—after all, you've never had me on your side before.'

'I'm still trying to work out whether that's an asset or a liability,' she retorted darkly. 'After all, you're the one who came up with this scheme in the first place. I must have been mad to agree.'

'Or madly in love,' he countered outrageously, and nearly stopped her heart. She'd thought that her feelings for him were her own private secret. Had she really been so obvious that he'd guessed...?

'Darling, I'd like you to meet the hospital chaplain,' he continued, smiling at someone approaching them along the corridor, and suddenly she understood that his startling words had been nothing more than part of the smokescreen concocted for her mother's benefit.

'Hello, Freya. Tom Bishop,' he said, holding out the hand that wasn't encumbered with the leather-bound book that, with the discreet white band at his neck, was the clear evidence of his calling. He turned to the woman who'd accompanied him. 'And this is Maura Frost, the local registrar, who comes in to deal with such things for the hospital. It took a bit of quick talking, but I managed to get your mother and her visitors to have a look at our little chapel, so if you're ready…'

'I'd better hand over the paperwork first,' Finn said as he shook the motherly-looking woman's hand then fished out an envelope from his inside pocket and handed it to her. 'If you'd like to check that's all in order before we go in? I'm sorry if we've inconvenienced both of you by doing everything at such short notice and in such a cloak-and-dagger way.'

'Well, it took a bit of arranging for a one-off permission to perform a marriage here and some people might think it's all a bit unorthodox. In this case I think it's a perfectly splendid idea,' the chaplain said with an approving smile for both of them that only made Freya feel more guilty. 'Not only will it help to take your mother's mind off the impending surgery, but I can imagine that the big family reception later on will give her something special to aim for when she's recuperating.'

Freya could see from the startled expression on Finn's face that that eventuality was something that he hadn't even considered. There wasn't time to talk about it now, though.

'I even took the liberty of bringing along my little camera, if you don't mind,' the cheerful little man continued. 'It's nice to be able to have mementoes of the happier occasions.'

'I'm glad you thought of it because it completely slipped my mind,' Finn admitted with a groan. 'Perhaps we can appoint you the official photographer and have two sets of prints made?'

'I'd be delighted.' He beamed. 'This day just gets better and better. Now, if Maura's happy with the paperwork and you're both ready, we can get this little surprise under way.' And he turned to approach the discreetly carved doors leading into the chapel.

For one desperate second Freya was certain that she wasn't going to be able to get her feet moving. Sheer terror had welded them to the slick utilitarian floor. Then Finn grasped her chilly hand between both of his.

'Ready?' he whispered, and her gaze was drawn up to meet the understanding expression in those green eyes.

Suddenly, she was bombarded with an absolute blizzard of whirling thoughts, every one of them registering faster than the speed of light.

First and foremost was the fact that she loved this man and had loved him ever since she'd met him. That should have made her glad that she was about to marry him, except for the major detail that he'd never mentioned love when he'd proposed.

Not that it had been a real proposal, in spite of the fact that he'd gone down on one knee in front of her. She was far too sensible to let herself think *that* performance had been anything more than a light-hearted joke.

Still, he'd seemed quite serious when he'd said that the success of their marriage was down to the commitment that the two of them were willing to put into it. That certainly sounded as if he intended their union to last longer than her pregnancy. Especially as he knew almost as well as she did her mother's views on divorce.

After all was said and done, it was her pregnancy that had precipitated the whole situation, and as he seemed to be willing to take on the responsibility— and her mother's eventual blame—for her otherwise illegitimate child...

'Chaplain, this was a lovely idea! Such a peaceful place in such a busy hospital,' Ruth exclaimed softly when she saw the man framed in the doorway. Freya, still out of sight in the corridor, had to smile. Her mother's bright vivacity completely belied the serious condition of her heart, almost as though she refused to admit to any weakness even when she was in hospital, waiting to undergo major surgery.

'Although I must tell you,' her mother continued briskly, 'I have every intention of surviving for many more years yet, so don't take it amiss if you're not my most favourite person. Now, Stuart, it's probably time I went back to my room or Freya won't know where to find me. She's due at any— Ah! There she is! At last!'

Freya's heart couldn't have been beating any faster if she'd been a mouse being chased by a cat. Any moment now she was going to hyperventilate and pass out in front of her whole family. Then her mother would be bound to ask some pointed questions.

'Where have you been all these weeks, sweetheart? Finn! You're here, too. Come in! Is it your fault she's been too busy to visit her family? And *your* parents are here, too. Oh, what pretty flowers! Are they for me?'

'Actually, Mum…' Freya interrupted, but her voice was almost too weak with nerves to be heard in the room.

She was amazed to find out just how much Finn had managed to organise in two weeks, but how on earth had he managed to get his parents to visit today without giving the game away?

'Actually, the flowers are for Freya,' Finn announced firmly, his deep voice effortlessly filling the peacefulness of that special room and drawing everyone's attention. 'We've arranged a little surprise to cheer you all up.'

'A surprise?' Ruth's eyes were suddenly uncomfortably intent as she scrutinised both of them from head to toe. They went from the bouquet held in Freya's trembling hands to the elegant cream silk suit—chosen to keep the beginnings of a bump at her waist hidden from prying eyes—to Finn's dark suit and the matching cream-coloured rose he'd slipped into his buttonhole.

'We're perfectly willing to wait until you're completely recovered before we have any sort of formal celebration,' Finn continued, 'but Freya and I didn't want to have to wait any longer before we actually tied the knot.'

'Tied the knot?' Ruth repeated, clearly completely taken aback. There were gasps from several of the gathered family members. 'You mean you're getting married? Here? Now?'

'With the help of Mr Bishop who kindly agreed to officiate and Mrs Frost, the registrar, who'll make sure it's all legal.'

There was a sudden explosion of exclamations as every member of the family tried to have their say. In the end it was the chaplain who called them to order with the ease of long practice.

'If the bride and groom would like to follow me up to the front,' he suggested with a gesture, 'and if Mrs Innes sits here, she'll have the best view of the proceedings.'

In a daze, Freya found herself complying, guided by Finn's hand at the back of her waist until they were standing side by side, with their families standing in a stunned semicircle around Ruth's wheelchair.

At that distance there was no way she could avoid the keen grey eyes so like her own. Even when she managed to drag her gaze away it was only to find

Astrid's thunderstruck expression, the bemused shake of her father's head or the strangely smug grin on Colum's face. As for Finn's parents, heaven only knew what they were making of the situation because she had no idea what he'd told them to get them here.

'Now, if we're all ready?' the chaplain asked, and opened up the leather-bound book at the place marked by a broad satin ribbon.

'Dearly beloved,' he began, his voice taking on an altogether more sonorous tone befitting the occasion. And suddenly the whole scene became very real for Freya, right down to Finn's hand reaching out to clasp her much smaller one in protective warmth.

When she gazed into those familiar green eyes she knew that, however they'd come to this situation, it felt right to be here with him, and a feeling of calm inevitability seemed to fill her.

She'd been afraid that guilt at the subterfuge they were perpetrating would mar the day. Then she looked up at the man who'd held her heart for six years, and as she promised to love and honour him she knew there was no deception involved. She was making the promises honestly and straight from her heart. The offer of marriage might have been precipitated by her mother's illness, but she was suddenly determined that she was going to do everything she could to fulfil her half of the bargain.

Her hand wasn't even shaking when she held it out for Finn to slip the ring she'd chosen on her finger, but she was startled when she had to do the same for him. It honestly hadn't occurred to her that he might want to have just as visible a sign of belonging as she had, and the very act of sliding the matching circle of gold on his finger did feel very possessive.

Mine, it seemed to say, and she couldn't help the little smile that curved her mouth at the fulfilment of so many of her dreams.

Then the chaplain said, 'You may kiss your bride.' And her heart nearly stopped altogether.

Her eyes flew up to meet Finn's and she wondered if he could read her sudden panic. She was supposed to kiss him? Now? In front of both their families? When she'd spent the last six years and countless joint family celebrations pretending that he meant no more to her than the fact that he was Astrid's brother-in-law?

For several long seconds they gazed at each other and she saw the mossy green of his eyes darken as he tilted his head towards her.

And then his lips met hers and she ceased to think at all.

She'd had dreams about that mouth…at first gentle, then persuasive and knowing, but ultimately utterly carnal and endlessly addictive…

A piercing whistle rent the air and Freya gasped in shock. She was even more stunned to open her eyes and meet the unexpected heat of desire blazing in Finn's cool green eyes and to realise that some time during their kiss he'd swept her up in his arms so that her feet didn't even meet the floor.

How could she not have noticed? she berated herself as he allowed her to slide slowly…far *too* slowly…down his body until her feet touched the floor again. He was so much taller than she was and yet she'd had her arms wrapped tightly around his neck, her fingers tangling in the thick tawny hair at the back of his head. Something should have told her that she…*they* were making an exhibition of themselves.

'Save some of that for later, little brother!' Colum exclaimed gleefully. 'Otherwise you're going to embarrass us all.'

Freya heard the others laughing and was vaguely aware of the flash of the chaplain's camera, but she still couldn't tear her eyes away from Finn and the maelstrom of expressions passing across his face.

He seemed almost surprised by their response to each other, but why that should be she had no idea. It was hardly likely that he'd been celibate during the years since they'd met. Even in the time that they'd been working together in A and E, she'd heard the intermittent gossip about who was his flavour of the month and more than a few sighs from those wishing he'd choose them. It had been hard not to notice that all of the more recently favoured ones had been tall, blonde and shapely—the absolute antithesis of her own petite darkness.

Admittedly, she hadn't heard about so many candidates since that fateful Emergency Care in the Community conference at the end of last year, but she'd put that down to the fact that he'd already exhausted the supply of available women at the hospital and was seeking company from other circles.

The fact that he'd never once asked her out but had seemed content with their involvement as wider members of the same family group had been a source of considerable pain, especially after the way she'd believed they'd connected in the aftermath of the conference.

How long they'd been standing there, gazing at each other, she didn't know, but suddenly she found herself plucked away from him and wrapped in Colum's arms.

'My turn,' he announced with a wide smile, and brushed a kiss over her cheek. 'I never thought that brother of mine would be so slow on the uptake. Still, I hope he's worth the wait. Welcome to the family.'

Freya hardly had time to thank him before Astrid had pushed him aside to sob happily in her ear.

'Now you're my sister *and* my sister-in-law, I think,' she declared as she sniffled into the hankie that Colum had produced without batting an eye.

'Hormones,' he muttered with an air of long-suffering.

Astrid scowled as she aimed an elbow at his ribs in retribution then rounded on Freya again.

'But you're so mean. Why didn't you give me a hint that this was going on between you and Finn? How long have the two of you been going out together? When did you start planning the wedding? Ours took months to arrange, so how on earth did you get it all brought forward at such short notice?'

Freya was frantically trying to formulate an answer that wouldn't give away the truth when another arm, stronger and longer, wrapped almost possessively around her shoulders.

'Don't you know that's one of the advantages of working in Accident and Emergency?' Finn declared. 'We're both well accustomed to working under pressure, so arranging a wedding was child's play, especially once we had the hospital chaplain and the registrar on our side.'

Tom Bishop had obviously picked up on the comment.

'I was delighted to be able to help out. It really cheers me up to be able to be part of one of life's more joyous occasions. I'm also available for christenings, if anyone's interested.'

Freya felt Finn grow tense even as she felt her smile freeze on her face. Neither of them had so much as hinted at the fact of her pregnancy. Had Tom Bishop somehow guessed at the basic reason for today's performance?

'We'll bear it in mind,' Astrid promised with a

pretty blush and a coy glance at Colum that left everyone open-mouthed.

'More grandchildren!' Finn's mother said, clearly delighted.

'Astrid!' Ruth exclaimed with a happy smile. 'Two celebrations in one day. You hadn't told me you were expecting again. When's it due, or is it twins again?'

'Good Lord, I hope not!' Stuart groaned, but there was no disguising his pleasure at the prospect of being a grandfather again. 'I hope you two will wait a bit before you start bombarding us with more grandchildren,' he said to Finn and Freya.

'Unlikely, if that kiss was any indication,' Colum muttered so that Ruth didn't hear him, his words apparently intended just for his brother's ears. With Finn's arm still firmly wrapped around her, Freya couldn't help but hear, and another blush quickly heated her face.

Before anyone could comment on it there was a brisk tap on the door.

'Right, now, people,' said the formidable senior nurse revealed by the open door, impressive in her immaculate dark blue uniform. 'My patient needs a bit of peace and quiet to get her strength up for tomorrow, so it's about time she went back to her room. Oh, Chaplain, I'm so sorry. I didn't know you were holding a service.'

'We finished a few minutes ago, nurse,' he said with a slightly smug smile. 'It's been a busy after-

noon. Spiritual counselling one minute, performing a
wedding the next, to say nothing of recording events
as the official photographer.' He held up the compact
camera as evidence. 'It's all part of the day when
you're doing the Lord's work.'

'A wedding?' she exclaimed, only then seeming to
see the pretty cream and white bouquet still clutched
in Freya's hand. 'Well, congratulations, I'm sure, but
I still need someone to take my patient back to her
room. I'll leave you to decide who it's going to be.'

'Well, I really ought to be getting on,' Tom Bishop
admitted, then turned to Finn and held up the little
camera. 'If you'd like to call in on your way out of
the hospital, I can let you have the film from this. I
think I got a couple of really good group shots, too.'

'I just need some signatures then I'll be out of
everyone's way,' Maura Frost said as she opened her
official ledger. 'Bride and groom first, please.'

'Then Astrid and I will go,' Colum volunteered,
ignoring his wife's disappointed pout as they waited
their turn to sign the register. 'That'll give Finn and
Freya a moment to speak to all the parents. Shall the
four of us meet up later?'

'Do you want to come over and have a meal with
us this evening?' Astrid invited eagerly. 'You could
spend the night if you like, so we can catch up on all
the details. You haven't seen the boys for a while
either.'

'I think we'll save that delight for tomorrow,

thanks,' Finn said with a grin as he exchanged a back-slapping hug with his older brother, then with his father and received a kiss from his slightly tearful mother. 'I've booked a room in a nearby hotel.'

'You haven't!' Ruth exclaimed. 'What on earth for? You and Freya will stay at home. I may not be there but Stuart will. A hotel? The very idea!'

'Or you could stay with us,' Finn's mother added eagerly. 'I know we're a little further away from the hospital but Finn's room has had a double bed in it ever since he topped six feet.'

'Actually...' Finn began hesitantly, and Freya knew he didn't want to hurt either mother's feelings. She also knew that her new husband was determined that they weren't going to be spending their first night with relatives. This whole charade was far too new to submit it to such close scrutiny.

'Hush, dear,' Finn's father said, clearly fighting a grin at Finn and Freya's badly hidden reticence. 'Of course they know they're welcome to stay with either of us any time, but this *is* the first night of their honeymoon, remember? The last thing they want is to be staying with their parents or in-laws.'

'Oh!' she exclaimed, and Freya was almost shocked to see Finn's elegant mother blush.

'Well, they're not going anywhere until I've given them both a hug,' Ruth declared, beckoning her daughter.

Freya stepped forward willingly. Her recent exile

from her family had been voluntary and entirely intended to spare her mother any upset. That didn't mean that she hadn't missed them all, especially the mother she'd unwittingly come so close to losing…could still lose if anything went wrong with her surgery tomorrow.

'Ah, Freya,' her mother said softly as she enveloped her in loving arms and the familiar scent of lavender. 'I'm so glad you found each other in the end. You've loved him for such a long time.'

Freya stiffened, pulling back just far enough to be able to see her mother's face and those very knowing eyes.

'You knew?' she breathed in shock, hoping desperately that her father and Finn's parents were talking loudly enough to stop Finn hearing this little confrontation. What had given her away? Did that mean that Finn knew, too? But, then, wouldn't he have said something when he'd proposed to her? Or would the fact that he didn't return the feeling have kept him silent? 'When did you find out? What gave it away?'

'I've always known,' she said complacently. 'Right from the first time I saw the two of you together.'

'But you never said anything? In all that time?'

Ruth rolled her eyes. 'It was hard to bite my tongue, but I knew that if it was meant to be, you would have to work it out for yourselves. You know I've tried hard not to be an interfering mother. Not that I wasn't tempted to give you a push a time or two...'

She gave Freya another hug then beckoned Finn over when she relinquished Freya to her father.

Finn's parents said their farewells as soon as they'd welcomed Freya to the family and extracted a promise of a visit in the near future, and then there were just the four of them left in the room.

Stuart led Freya across to stand in relative seclusion beside a window looking out across a peaceful stretch of garden bright with summer blooms.

'I know Finn's a good man, but this has all happened in such a rush. Are you happy, little one?' he demanded softly, obviously being careful that his words didn't carry.

'You're right about everything happening in a rush. At the moment my head's still spinning too much to know how I'm feeling,' Freya said evasively, easily able to avoid meeting the eyes of her much taller father.

He chuckled. 'Well, I'll say the same thing to you as I said to Finn. Your mother, God bless her, would deny with her last breath that she's afraid she'll never wake up from this surgery. I'm glad that the two of you came to visit her and that you cared enough to want to set her mind at rest about you in particular. Now she'll be going into the operating theatre tomorrow knowing that both her chicks are settled and happy. That means a great deal to her—to both of us.'

Freya felt the hot press of tears behind her eyes as her guilt rose up to haunt her anew. Everyone was saying such lovely things about her marriage to Finn when the whole thing was just an elaborate performance cobbled together at the last minute to ease her mother's mind. The fact that she loved her new husband wasn't really a factor, except to her.

'Oh, Dad,' she whispered huskily as she accepted his hug.

'Oh, Lord,' he groaned theatrically. 'You were always the sensible one. Don't tell me marriage is going to turn you into a watering can just like your sister. I couldn't stand it. Finn,' he called urgently, 'take this woman away before she starts crying all over me. From now on, mopping up her tears is your responsibility.'

Her father's words were still echoing in Freya's head as Finn drove them away from the hospital.

In a way they had simplified her thoughts but, in so doing, they had also presented her with the prospect of future heartbreak.

Yes, Finn *was* a good man, a caring man—the fact that he'd married her at all was proof of that. But would he ever love her, *could* he ever love her, and if not, would caring be enough for a lifetime together, especially when there were still so many unanswered questions about Finn's feelings towards her?

The dainty bouquet was still clutched tightly in Freya's hand when they finally drew up in front of the impressive façade of the country hotel.

For just a moment she'd been tempted to put them in a vase of water in her mother's hospital room. Then, when her hand had hovered over it, she'd been unable to relinquish her hold on the combination of fragile white baby's breath, innocent creamy roses and scented white lavender.

No standard hospital forecourt bouquet this, but one that Finn had specially ordered at some time in the last two weeks and that he'd presented to her before they'd driven to her mother's hospital.

Somehow she hadn't been able to make herself plunge the stems in water, much though the blooms needed some respite from the tight grasp of her nervous hand. And so, here they were, slightly the worse for wear but a tangible reminder of the unbelievable events of the last few hours.

The only other visible reminder was the ring now gleaming softly on her finger, yet another example of Finn's attention to detail.

Freya had been fully prepared to press her grandmother's ring into service—had actually taken it out of her little jewellery case to suggest it to Finn when he'd surprised her with a visit to a jeweller near the hospital.

Not only had Finn remembered the necessity for a ring but he'd even warned the jeweller that he would need a selection dainty enough to suit her slender hands. What he hadn't done was tell her that he was going to buy a matching one for himself at the same time, and somehow that omission accentuated the fact that she still had much to learn about him.

'Well, Dr Wylie, here we are,' he announced in the sudden silence as he switched off the engine. 'Are you ready to go in and find something to eat?'

Dr *Wylie*? she thought with a sudden spurt of amazement mixed with a glimmer of humour. There were two of them now. That could be fun in the department when they were both on duty together. Thank goodness they were all on first-name terms.

'Yes, Dr Wylie, I believe I am,' she responded with a grin that widened into outright laughter when her stomach suddenly rumbled.

Long, sleepless hours later Finn lay on his side, beside his new wife with his head propped up on one hand.

He'd been lying there for some time watching the way the soft buttery light of her forgotten bedside lamp gilded the pale perfection of Freya's elfin face and highlighted the tumbled profusion of her darkly spiralling hair.

He'd known she was apprehensive about sharing a room with him, could tell by the way she'd avoided even the simplest of touches while they'd unpacked their minimal belongings before heading down to the dining room.

At the end of the meal she'd eagerly agreed to his suggestion that they take a turn around the stunning gardens. She'd even seemed to relax a little when they'd found a secluded wooden bench with a panoramic view of patchwork fields and woodland that seemed to stretch over several counties.

Then, even though the summer evenings seemed to linger for ever as the solstice approached, it had been time to go back to their room.

They were hardly inside the door when she bolted for the bathroom with her wash-bag. When she finally emerged he barely had time for anything more than a glance at a delightfully skimpy cotton nightdress before she was pulling the covers up to her chin.

He took his time under the shower, turning the temperature gradually colder as he remembered that brief glimpse of surprisingly long slender legs and a curvaceous body tantalisingly silhouetted against the light behind her.

He was determined to have all evidence of his body's reaction to her under control before he joined her in that bed, and equally determined to make sure that she understood she didn't have anything to fear from him. She wasn't to know that he'd been keeping his emotions under strict control for the last six years, but he could certainly reassure her that another few days or weeks wouldn't be a problem if that was what she would prefer.

He'd even been resigned to the possibility that it might be months until she felt comfortable with the idea of consummating their marriage, but once they'd kissed in the chapel…once he'd felt her response to nothing more than his mouth on hers…he'd known that it wouldn't take much to fan that spark of attraction.

It certainly wasn't going to be happening tonight, he thought with a stifled groan, trying to ignore his body's urgent demands. He came out of the bathroom with a thick towel wrapped around his waist to disguise the response that refused to be frozen into submission, only to find that he needn't have bothered.

Far from lying there in fear and trepidation that he was about to summarily jump her bones, Freya was sleeping with all the innocent abandon of a child. And here he was, several hours later, still lying here watching his wife while she slept.

In this soft light her face was so relaxed that he could see how tense she'd been over the last few weeks. Like this, it was hard to reconcile the fact that she was twenty-nine with the youthful appearance of her porcelain skin. She didn't seem to have aged a day since he'd met her.

Suddenly he wondered if the child she carried would take after her or the unknown man who'd fathered him.

He wasn't proud of the sharp twist of jealousy that knotted his insides when he thought of his Freya in another man's arms. She *was* his now, by virtue of the ceremony in which they'd taken part today, but as far as he was concerned she'd been his ever since the first time he'd taken her slender hand in his and gazed into those wide grey eyes.

For the first time in his life it hadn't mattered that she'd been Colum's date and that his brother might have been madly in love with her. From that first second, something inside him had recognised her and had growled, *Mine.*

She turned over and he held his breath for a moment, worried that she might wake up and find him watching her. Would she be unnerved by his scrutiny or find it flattering?

The bedclothes had become twisted and dislodged by her movement and Finn's eyes took in the geography of her new position, the new fullness of her breasts outlined faithfully by the fine fabric of her nightdress. Her body seemed just as slender as ever so was it just his imagination that he could see the growing mound of the child developing inside her? Was she already aware of the fledgling movements that detailed the progress of that development? Would he be able to feel the child moving if he put his hand there?

The idea of feeling Freya's child moving inside her stopped his thoughts in their tracks.

He honestly didn't know which he wanted more—
to feel the child moving, knowing it was a part of the
woman who was now his wife, or to resent its very
existence as proof that she'd once loved someone else
enough to share her body with him.

Careful not to disturb her, he lay back on his own
pillow and closed his eyes while he pondered the apparently insoluble dilemma.

In the end, just as he was finally slipping into sleep,
he decided that having a pregnant Freya in his life
was better than having no Freya at all. It was only
the green worm of jealousy that made him want to
demand the name of the man responsible.

CHAPTER SIX

FREYA had gone to sleep determined to stay on her own side of the bed, but woke up to find herself plastered against Finn's nakedness from head to foot.

It was bad enough that her head was tucked comfortably onto his shoulder and one arm was wrapped around the impressive width of his chest. The unforgivable intimacy was that some time in the night she'd inserted a possessive leg across his powerfully muscled thighs and her knee was nudging the indisputable evidence that his was now a very aroused naked body.

She froze, wondering how on earth she was going to get herself out of this situation.

Obviously, there was no way she was going to be able to peel herself off him without waking him. Too many years of sleeping with one eye open when on call meant they were both all too adept at waking with at least half of their brain cells working the moment they surfaced. They had to be if they were going to be ready to deal with the next emergency.

Anyway, she didn't really know whether he *was* still asleep. She'd heard enough raunchy conversations from her fellow female colleagues to know that most healthy men woke up in such a condition, but this was certainly much more…um…*potent* than she'd been expecting from someone who was still asleep.

But, then, what did she know? In spite of her twenty-nine years, this was the first time she'd ever woken up in bed with a man—in fact, it was only the second time she'd been *in* a bed with a man and look what had happened as the result of the first time.

Well, she was going to have to move soon. There was a bathroom just a few steps away and with the pressure the growing baby was exerting on her internal organs, there wasn't nearly the same liquid capacity.

So, the decision was made. Speed was the answer. She was going to take a deep breath then she was going to slide straight out of the bed and sprint out of sight behind the bathroom door before he had a chance to open his eyes.

Ready…steady…

'Good morning, Freya,' Finn rumbled in a sleep-rusty voice, and she barely stopped herself from groaning out loud. She certainly couldn't bring herself to look at him.

Great! *Now* how was she supposed to untangle herself from his…his tangible assets…to make her exit from the room? Why couldn't he have stayed asleep for just another minute? Another thirty seconds would have done. Just till she was out of bed and out of sight.

'I wondered how long you were going to sleep,' he continued, his voice sounding as lazy and relaxed as a big cat's purr.

'How long have you been awake?' she demanded weakly, feeling the searing heat of a blush spread right up her throat and into her cheeks when she remembered where her leg was lodged. At least her hair covered most of her face even if it had to resemble a giant rats' nest.

'Not long,' he said, then slid a hand nonchalantly under the covers to lift her encroaching knee aside and roll away to sit up on the edge of the bed. 'Sorry about that. Fact of nature,' he said dismissively as he retrieved a towel from somewhere out of her sight and wound it strategically around his waist.

Stung by a sudden fit of pique that he could be so glib, and determined that she wasn't going to let herself admire the contrast between the white towel and the toasty golden colour of his skin, she was aghast to hear herself challenge him.

'So it had nothing to do with my presence in the bed?'

The fierce expression in his eyes when he half turned to face her had her wishing even more fervently that she'd kept her mouth shut.

'You're hardly innocent at nearly five months pregnant so you should know better than that,' he said gruffly, and she was almost certain that she could hear a strange underlying layer of pain in his voice. 'Surely your baby's father must have woken up like that a time or two.'

'My baby's father?' she repeated blankly, shock robbing her of the wit or the breath to say more.

'Well, I know there must be one because you wouldn't have deliberately become pregnant by artificial insemination. Not outside marriage, anyway. Unless it was an unexpected, more casual encounter…?'

'But…' Her brain still wasn't functioning properly and her heart seemed to have stopped completely…or was it just pounding so fast that she couldn't count the beats? Was he really implying that there was any doubt who had fathered her child? What sort of a promiscuous person did he think she was? And he'd *married* her harbouring such thoughts?

'So, are we going to have to go through any legal shenanigans to have my name put on the birth certificate?' he grated, the usual soft mossy green of his eyes now seeming as hard as malachite as they bored into hers. 'Or has he already relinquished all claims?'

Freya felt sick. Never in her wildest nightmares had she imagined this conversation.

'B-but you *know* who the father is,' she stammered, her teeth almost chattering with shock as she took in the implications of what he was saying. Panic loosened the knots in her tongue and words began to pour out disjointedly. 'We went to that conference…you remember? The first one after I joined the team…the Emergency Health Care one in France… Then the airport was closed on the way back because of freezing fog.'

'And we had to take the ferry instead,' he said with a grimace. 'Otherwise we wouldn't have got back in time for the twins' birthday party. Yes, I remember that, but what's it got to do with…? You mean, the father was someone you met at the conference? But…but you'd never even met any of them before!'

He looked completely stunned by the idea, but no more than she was that he should even think her capable of such behaviour. Especially when he knew better. Especially when he knew…

All of a sudden her brain started working properly, putting nearly five months of disappointment and speculation together with the revelations of this latest conversation. It was impossible—beyond contemplation—that Finn would deliberately lie about something so serious. But if that was so, there must be another answer.

She'd wondered at his strange reticence since that trip—the continuing brotherly camaraderie—but had never imagined that there might be something more than the fact that he was simply ignoring what had happened. Had some shock actually robbed him of all recall?

'So…' she began as nausea started to roil through

her, the way it hadn't for a couple of months now. This was a minefield that needed careful negotiation. 'You remember the conference?'

'Of course I remember the conference,' he snapped impatiently. 'I'm hardly senile at thirty-four. I just don't remember you cosying up enough with any of the delegates to end up pregnant.'

'Cosying up?' she repeated, her cautious approach shot to pieces by a sudden explosion of anger. 'You make me sound like some cheap tart out for her thrills wherever she can find them. In case you've forgotten, my profession is as a doctor, not a hooker.'

At least he had the grace to look remorseful.

'I'm sorry, Freya. I'm sorry. That didn't come out the way I meant it. I only meant... Ah, hell!' He raked stiff fingers through tousled tawny hair. 'You're tying me up in knots when you know damned well that I don't think of you like that. I only wanted to make sure that some other man wasn't going to come barging in and upsetting everything when we'd gone to so much effort to make sure your mother wasn't stressed.'

Freya's anger subsided like a tired balloon. She did know that Finn hadn't intended to insult her but it had been such a shock to hear him say that he didn't know who had fathered her baby.

How was that possible?

Marcel, one of the organisers of the conference,

had arranged for the whole British contingent to be taken to the ferry to complete their journey home.

At Finn's insistence, he'd even managed to secure a cabin for him, in spite of the relatively short crossing time, as the two of them had wanted the chance to shower and change before they arrived at the twins' birthday party.

Liam, an anaesthetist colleague of Finn's from their training days who'd attended the conference *en route* from an exchange stint in a French hospital, had even sat chatting to Finn for a few minutes before joining some of the others in search of a hot meal.

There was something completely crazy going on here, and she wasn't going to be able to work it out while she was staring up over acres of lean tanned muscles into those green eyes.

It had been far too disconcerting to see the genuine puzzlement in those eyes when she'd said that he knew who the father was. And he *should* know, unless…

Freya closed her eyes a moment, forcing herself to recall those few moments as accurately as possible. There was something nagging at the back of her memory…

Liam had brought a bag into the room with him— a traditional doctor's bag that he was leaving with them for safety lest someone on the ferry took a fancy to it for the few basic drugs it contained—and he'd just been locking it when Freya had come into the tiny cabin. And Finn... Finn had been rubbing his thigh, almost as if...as if he'd just been given an injection?

Suddenly, it was as if a bright light had been switched on in a dark place.

'Have you ever gone sailing?' she demanded sharply, only realising just how sharply when she saw him blink.

'A couple of times. Why?'

'Did you enjoy it?' She was almost humming with the nervous tension building inside her.

'Yes and no. Look, what's this got to do with—?'

'Why didn't you enjoy it?' she probed eagerly. 'I would have thought it was right up your street. You're big and strong and into all those outdoor things like hiking and climbing. And didn't Colum have his own boat until the twins came along? Didn't you go sailing with him?'

'As I said, I only went a couple of times and I enjoyed the physical challenge of it, too,' he admitted. 'It was the nausea I couldn't take.'

'You get seasick,' she said as several more pieces of the puzzle slotted into place.

'Vilely,' he groaned. 'The balance mechanism in my ears is hypersensitive, for some unknown reason, and the amount of sedation it takes to stop me from being sick also completely stops me from being able to sail.'

'So you wouldn't have taken the ferry if you'd had a choice.'

'Never,' he said fervently. 'In fact, if Liam hadn't had his bag with him I probably wouldn't have been in a fit state to go to the twins' birthday party. He gave me a shot of quick-acting anti-emetic before the ferry set off.'

He mentioned the name of the drug and the last piece of the puzzle clicked home.

The substance Liam had administered to stop Finn being sick had a relatively short half-life, which would have made it ideal for controlling nausea for such a comparatively brief trip. Unfortunately, it was also well known for causing spells of amnesia while it was in effect. So it seemed as if Finn literally had no memory of anything that had happened in the cabin after the drug began to work.

Not that the knowledge would be any help to Freya in her present predicament. Her detective work might have solved one mystery but it had left her with an even bigger one—deciding whether to fill in the blanks in Finn's memory and, if so, how and when.

'Dammit,' Finn cursed as the icy water pounded down on him from the oversized showerhead. 'How could everything have gone wrong so quickly?'

He'd been having another one of those dreams when he'd woken up…the erotic ones that featured a naked water-slick Freya wrapped around his body while she urged him to make mad, passionate love to her. And he'd woken up to find that, for the first time, part of the dream had come true. She might not have been naked and water-slick, and she was unfortunately still asleep, but Freya was definitely wrapped around his naked body. His painfully aroused naked body.

It had seemed strangely familiar to see the way the long spirals of her dark hair had tumbled over her shoulder to mix with his dark tawny pelt, and her hand had looked impossibly pale and slender against the expanse of his chest. And as for the intimate position of her leg...

He'd lain there for a century or two, alternately savouring and suffering the situation while he waited for her to wake.

Deep inside he'd hoped that she'd realise where she was and what was happening, and that she'd invite him to live out the fantasies that seemed to have been filling his head for months. Realistically he'd been more certain that as soon as she woke she'd be trying to find a polite way to put as much distance between them as possible.

Well, he'd certainly got that right.

He'd known the instant she'd realised the state of his body because she'd gone as rigid as a steel bar against him. Turning away from her had been the only way he could think of to save them both embarrassment. Except that his male ego had kicked in with that crazy demand to know who had fathered her baby and she'd nearly gone into orbit.

Then, out of the blue, she'd started asking him about his preferences in sports…as if his skill at sailing had anything to do with the conversation. He'd grown accustomed to his brother's jibes over the years, but just for a moment she'd seemed strangely pleased when she'd discovered that he'd needed chemical help just to cross the English Channel.

Then the crazy woman had dropped the conversation altogether and had taken herself off to the bathroom, only emerging when she was fully dressed in a silky floral summer dress in some floaty fabric that reached almost to her ankles.

Imagining the petite delights he now knew were camouflaged under the blue and lilac herbaceous border she was wearing was the reason he was suffering through yet another long cold shower. At this rate he'd be the only man in the known universe to suffer from frostbite in the middle of summer.

And they still needed to sit down and talk about the united front they were going to have to present to their combined families.

Perhaps when breakfast arrived—any minute now if the man on the other end of the phone was right about the efficiency of room service—they'd be able to begin the conversation again a little more calmly and rationally.

In the meantime, he'd chosen boxer shorts and his

loosest pleated-front chinos to wear today, knowing damned well that spending the whole day with the real Freya was going to be almost as constantly and frustratingly uncomfortable as dreaming about the fantasy one.

Freya had never been more grateful for a strong pair of male arms while she waited to hear the results of her mother's surgery.

She and Finn had managed a stilted conversation over the enormous cooked breakfast he'd ordered— he'd actually finished the half she hadn't been able to manage without any effort *and* had looked as if he'd challenge her for the last few bites of her toast—and they'd set out a sketchy plan of campaign.

When they'd finally arrived at the hospital, at least an hour earlier than expected, they'd discovered that Ruth had already been taken to Theatre because a previous case had been deemed unwell enough for anaesthetic.

At that point, having realised that she was too late to give her mother a last kiss for luck, Freya had started to come a little unravelled at the seams.

In the event, it wasn't playacting that had her turning to Finn for comfort, and it didn't feel as if it was just because he was sticking to their plan that he'd wrapped her tightly against his side while she fought tears.

'Your mother was sorry not to see you before they

took her down,' Stuart said softly. 'But she refused to let me ring you to warn you what was happening.'

'But why?' Freya demanded, more hurt than she could say. Was it because she hadn't visited for so long that her mother had thought she wouldn't want to be here?

Finn must have heard something of her distress in her voice that made him tighten his hold on her. Suddenly, in spite of the glorious summer weather outside and the constant temperature the hospital maintained inside, she needed his warmth to ward off the chill of exclusion.

'Only because she said it was the wrong thing to do when you might be…um…after the first night of anyone's honeymoon,' he explained with an endearing touch of discomfort, as though the idea of his youngest child indulging in anything of *that* nature was somehow embarrassing. 'She was actually hoping she would already be in Recovery by the time you got here so you could arrive to good news.'

'So she's been in surgery much longer than they expected?' Freya's imagination was already conjuring up the worst. 'Have they struck a problem? Has someone been out to tell you what's going on?'

'It's probably nothing more than the fact they couldn't get her to shut up long enough to administer the anaesthetic and get the mask on her,' Stuart said wryly. 'She was probably trying to persuade them to let her supervise, just to make sure they did a good job.'

'Dad!' Astrid exclaimed thickly, her eyes already red from weeping and a soggy hankie clutched in her hand. 'You shouldn't say things like that.'

'Why not, when they're true?' he said cheerfully, displaying a deep knowledge of his partner of nearly thirty-five years. 'The fact that she's come in for surgery isn't going to change her nature. She's always been the type to take care of everyone else and to lend a hand if they need it. She certainly wouldn't see the incongruity in trying to organise her own surgery.'

Freya could feel Finn chuckling beside her before the sound reached her, the taut muscles of his stomach tightening against her.

'I can just imagine it,' he said with a broad grin. 'She'd probably start by asking if they'd all washed their hands properly, just like she does with the twins at mealtimes.'

Astrid gave a watery chuckle, just as the door to the waiting room swished open to admit a slightly rumpled figure in surgical greens.

'Just a quick visit to tell you all went well,' said the surgeon with a smile. 'We didn't find any surprises, so her recovery should be pretty straightforward.'

'Provided I can find a way to nail her foot to the floor,' Stuart retorted as he shook Peter Donaldson's hand, but Freya could see the glimmer of relieved tears in his pale blue eyes.

The strength of her parents' marriage had been a constant bulwark in the life of their family, but she was only now realising that the relationship between the two of them was the ideal against which she'd measured all her fledgling attempts.

How strange that it had taken till now, when she was already married to Finn Wylie, that she should finally understand what she'd been looking for all these years and why.

Unfortunately, she had no idea whether her hastily contrived arrangement had just condemned the two of them to a lifetime of misery rather than the supportive union her parents had achieved.

'When can we see her, Peter?' Stuart asked. 'Will she be up to having visitors?'

'She won't be settled in ICU for another half-hour or so and I'd rather you were the only visitor for the next twenty-four hours. Even then, you'll only be able to sit with her for ten minutes every hour until we see how she goes.'

'The usual, in other words,' Stuart said dryly. 'Well, as long as I get to see for myself that she's doing all right.'

'And no pestering the nurses to show you all her charts,' the surgeon warned with a comradely twinkle. 'They've got enough to do without spending half their day keeping you up to date with every entry on the temperature chart. You'll have to trust me to tell you if there's anything you need to know.'

'Fair enough,' Stuart agreed, holding his hand out again. 'And thank you for what you've done for Ruth.'

'My pleasure,' Peter said, and with a brief salute for the rest of them he strode back out into the corridor.

Astrid was sobbing quietly into a hankie again, this time tears of relief, but Freya was quite happy to be held tightly in Finn's arms.

'Well, thank God that part's over,' Stuart said with a relieved sigh that seemed to come all the way from the soles of his feet. 'Now, you lot are welcome to keep me company until I go up to ICU, but you might just as well go back home for now.'

'Are you sure, Dad? Finn and I don't have anything planned for the rest of the day, so we could stay,' Freya offered, not liking the thought that they were abandoning him to the wait alone.

'Actually, I was thinking of making my way to the hospital chapel for a few minutes,' he explained. 'The chaplain called in to see your mother before she had her pre-med and said that, barring any emergencies, he'd be there all afternoon if I wanted a chat. Nice chap.'

'Well, we'd better get back to our two monsters before they dismember the babysitters,' Colum announced. 'Be sure to tell Ruth we wish her well as soon as she's *compos mentis* enough to understand.'

'Will do. And thanks for being here with me.' Stuart clapped Colum on the shoulder and gave Astrid a hug then turned to Freya and Finn. 'And as for you two, it's time for you to get back to enjoying your honeymoon, such as it is. I hope you're intending to organise something a bit better as soon as all this fuss is over. Although I have to warn you, Ruth has already started making lists of all the people she's going to invite to the reception she's planning. She reckons she'll be ready to stage it in a matter of weeks, but I was suggesting a couple of months, just to be on the safe side. We don't want any stress to cause a setback.'

'You tell her to concentrate on getting better. There's plenty of time to think about organising parties,' Finn said breezily before they made their farewells.

Freya just wanted to laugh and there would have been more than a hint of hysteria to it if she gave in to the urge. She really hoped her mother *hadn't* got her heart set on a fancy reception. If the time it had taken to organise Astrid's wedding was any guide, by the time all the arrangements were finalised it could end up doing double duty as a christening party.

'Where do you want to go?' Finn asked when they climbed back into his car.

Freya rubbed both hands over her face while she tried to order her thoughts.

'I really don't know,' she admitted in the end. 'One part of me wants to lie down quietly in a darkened room, but the other part is so zizzed up with everything that's been going on in the last couple of weeks that I feel I could go hot-air ballooning without needing the gas burner.'

'Well, at least you know that the operation's over and your mother's on the mend, so that's one worry less,' he pointed out.

'The other one's still hanging over my head like the sword of Damocles, in a manner of speaking. I was just trying to imagine everyone's reaction if I came to the reception they're planning dressed in a tent and proceeded to go into labour just when it's time to cut the cake.'

'Now, *that* would make an impact,' he agreed with a groan. 'Still, as I said to your father, there's plenty of time for all that. Let's concentrate on today. How about finding somewhere nice and quiet where we can sit with a pot of tea and some disgustingly fattening cakes and watch the world go by?'

'If you could manage to throw in a view of water somewhere in that scenario, you're on.'

He drove out of the car park to head out of town and they ended up meandering randomly from village to village, drawn purely by the more interesting or outlandish names.

At one point they found a little stream trickling and glittering its way over the well-washed stones of a ford. Freya could imagine that in full winter spate it would probably be a couple of feet deep, but at the moment, in midsummer, it was picture perfect.

She glanced across at Finn and found him waiting to meet her eyes, and without a word being spoken he drove a little further and found a place to park.

They'd walked a little way upstream to find a place to sit with their feet in the water and for nearly an hour they sat in the dappled shade and talked about nothing in particular.

In spite of their underlying concern about Ruth, their day continued in the same strangely mellow mood right up to the moment when the waiter asked if they wanted another cup of coffee at the end of their meal.

Once again there was that wordless communication between them before they both shook their heads and opted for another stroll in the garden, but now she was aware of a slender thread of tension which had started to tighten between them.

Then Finn threaded his fingers between hers and Freya was certain she must have been mistaken. She even had to subdue the sappy grin that threatened to take over her face when she realised that the whole afternoon had felt like a first innocent date might have done if she'd met Finn when she'd been a teenager.

Her heart was dancing silly jigs inside her chest

when she realised how far they'd come in just twenty-four hours. Last night they'd barely come close enough to speak, let alone hold hands. Was this a significant step forward or did it merely mean that, in spite of the good report their recent phone call had received of her mother's condition, Finn was merely offering silent support?

Whatever it was, he didn't seem to be in any hurry to break the contact and she certainly didn't want to. The idea of walking together in a beautiful garden at the end of the day was something she'd only dreamed about over the last six years, and when she allowed herself to remember that they would be spending the night together, in the same bed...

If she wasn't careful she was going to start hyper-ventilating, especially when she pictured the way she'd ended up wrapped around him that morning. And for all his nonchalance when he'd extricated himself, she wasn't nearly so sure that he'd been as unaffected as he'd tried to tell her.

Was that the way to build the relationship between them? She'd always believed that it was important for a couple to get to know each other in the ordinary sense before they progressed to the biblical, but surely their case was different?

Her thoughts were still going round and round the same basic subject when they reached the bench with the stunning view, but this time when they sat down

Finn wrapped an arm around her shoulders and pulled her close into the curve of his body.

It seemed almost automatic to angle her head so it rested on the comfortable width of his chest, and when she breathed in she didn't just recognise the perfume of the night-scented stock nearby but also the familiar mixture of soap and man that was unique to Finn.

This was what she wanted, she thought fervently, this closeness that needed no busy conversation to sustain it. How many times had she come across her parents sitting silently together and wondered why they weren't speaking? She'd never realised before that sometimes words were completely unnecessary.

And if she and Finn had already progressed this quickly from a state of near war to tranquil peace, did that mean they were ready for a more radical step?

They were already married and had made a public commitment to stay together, not least for the sake of the baby. She knew they had a long way to go to build a strong marriage—the sort that would withstand anything that a lifetime could throw at it. It didn't help that an essential element of the link between them had been lost to the side-effect of something as unexciting as an anti-emetic.

So, if their marriage were to be consummated…if, instead of clinging to her edge of the mattress and hoping for sleep, she were to turn to him and welcome his body's natural reaction to being in bed with her...

Would that help to build the bonds between them and strengthen them, or was that just her rioting hormones talking?

By the time they were meandering their way back to the mellow brick building she was more than halfway to convincing herself that deepening the physical aspects of their relationship was a good idea.

As they went up in the lift she wished fleetingly that she'd had time to read some of the more explicit novels her sister had passed her way, but it was too late now. In a matter of minutes they were going to be in their room and they were going to get undressed and climb into that bed again. Together. It was a thought that had desire coiling deep inside her, but it was also terrifying to realise that if she was going to try to seduce Finn she was going to have to rely on her imagination.

He was ushering her through the door with a guiding hand warm at the back of her waist when she sent up one last despairing thought.

Please, Finn, take the initiative as soon as you realise that I'm willing.

CHAPTER SEVEN

THE first thing Freya saw as she entered the room still lit with the soft pinks and apricots of the fading day was the blinking message light on the phone.

'Oh, Finn. Has something happened to Mum?' For a moment she was frozen by fear, hardly daring to approach the instrument.

'Unlikely, in such a short space of time,' Finn said, automatically reassuring her as he strode across to pick up the receiver. It only took a few seconds for him to access the message and set her mind at rest.

'It's from St David's, Freya, not the General,' he said as he began to tap out the familiar number with a scowl. 'And whoever thought they were going to interrupt our three days off has got another think coming. I even left my mobile behind so we wouldn't be disturbed.'

He glanced across at her and threw her one of those wicked smiles that had always sent her pulse crazy. 'Why don't you take advantage of the bathroom first? If I finish in time I could come in and scrub your back, if you like.'

Freya felt her eyes widen at the blatantly flirtatious tone. Was it possible that she hadn't been the only one thinking about changing the parameters of their hasty union? While they'd been sitting together, looking out over the beautiful countryside, had Finn been coming to the same conclusions?

Her heart gave a series of thumps loud enough to be heard on the other side of the room and she whirled quickly to grab her nightdress.

On her way to the bathroom she was wishing futilely that she'd brought something infinitely sexier to wear if she was going to try her hand at seduction for the first time. Suddenly, Finn swore sharply and stopped her in her tracks.

'What's the matter?' She turned back, knowing there was something seriously wrong because he wasn't one for gratuitous bad language.

'Turn the television on and you'll probably see,' he directed, obviously waiting impatiently to be connected to someone.

Freya grabbed the remote control and pressed the first button she came to, wondering what on earth was happening. Almost instantly the screen was filled with a scene of carnage.

'...all this the result of a light aircraft crashing into a bridge spanning the motorway,' the reporter was saying, while behind him smoke and flames rose from dozens of vehicles damaged and destroyed by the ensuing mayhem.

'Dear God...' she whispered, sinking onto the corner of the bed, her eyes riveted to the scene unfolding in front of the camera's eye. 'When did this happen? Where?'

'A little more than halfway between here and the hospital. They've sent out messages for as many off-duty staff who can get there to come in. Unfortunately, the roads you're seeing on the screen are our two main options for getting there.'

'Which hospital? Mum's or ours?' Freya's brain was still being overloaded by the images she was watching.

'Ours, but I've no idea how they found out we were here. Do you suppose they contacted our families?' He didn't need a reply from her as his connection had finally gone through on the phone.

Freya only had to hear one half of the conversation to realise that the situation was desperate, with every available trained body needed. A quick glance down at her long summer dress was enough to remind her that she certainly wasn't dressed for the job. Without a thought for the fact that Finn could see what she was doing, she swiftly stripped it off over her head and replaced it with the cotton drawstring trousers and sleeveless tunic top she'd intended wearing in the morning.

By the time Finn had finished the last in a quickfire series of calls she was stuffing the last of their belongings in their bags and was ready to go.

'Good girl,' he said with a distracted smile. 'We've got to get to the General now. There are so many casualties that they're taking half, with helicopters and ambulances running constant relays in both directions.'

'But if the roads are closed, how are we going to get there? It was all right wandering around all those tiny country roads this afternoon, but it would take far too long to find our way through them in a hurry, especially once it gets really dark.'

'According to the policeman I spoke to, it's going to be a case of getting to the General then hitching a ride on one of the emergency vehicles,' he said, his long legs already eating up the distance to the main staircase.

Freya resigned herself to running along in his wake. With his mind already on the task ahead, there was no way he was going to remember that his legs were so much longer than hers. Thank goodness he was carrying their bags or she'd have been left completely behind.

Organised chaos was a good way of describing the scene that met their eyes when they tried to approach the General.

Apart from the constant stream of emergency vehicles making their way to and from the casualty entrance, there seemed to be an enormous volume of other traffic jamming up the area.

'Who are all these people?' Freya demanded, while Finn tried to manoeuvre between a large white van with a logo on the side and a tight knot of pedestrians. Until he could find somewhere to park he couldn't begin to track down the man who was going to try to arrange for their transportation.

Finn's patience finally ran out and he tapped his horn briefly to remind the pedestrians that they were blocking the traffic.

'Do you mind, mate?' snarled one man as he whirled to glare at them at short distance. 'Can't you see we're trying to record a story here!'

Freya gasped at the sheer effrontery and wasn't in the least surprised when Finn responded with a renewed and far more strident blast of his horn.

'Look, mate! I already *told* you to wait,' the reporter shouted, this time right beside Finn's window. 'I'm recording the news here!'

As Finn wound the window down just far enough so the self-obsessed film-maker could hear him speak, they could both hear the sound of yet another ambulance wailing its way ever closer.

'And I'm telling you to shift this circus before you become one of the casualties yourself,' Finn snapped.

'Who the hell do you think you are?' the newsman sneered dismissively. 'I've got the freedom of the press and this is news.'

'And I'm the doctor who'll make certain that you're the very *last* person to be treated if you're run over by the next ambulance,' Finn threatened in a steely voice that actually made the obnoxious man take a step back from the window. 'And I'll also make certain you're arrested and charged with obstruction if you and your van aren't out of the way in thirty seconds.'

With that parting shot he wound up the window and reapplied his hand to the horn.

'If looks could kill,' Freya murmured, watching the hurried way the film crew piled their equipment and themselves back into the white van with the station logo on the side, then screeched out of the emergency reception area.

'No doubt they'll be back as soon as they've found somewhere close by to park,' he said wryly. 'I just hope they'll give me long enough to be out of the way, or I might actually have to do what I promised.'

Freya laughed, although there really wasn't anything remotely funny in the situation. Still, she could just imagine how intimidated the arrogant man had been. Finn's height and build were fairly obvious even when he was sitting in a car, and with his favourite leather jacket on, battered from years of use and the glacial expression in both eyes and voice, it was no wonder the man had backed down in a hurry.

Luckily, once the journalists were out of the way it was relatively easy for Finn to find the staff car park that he'd been told to use, and within minutes they were hurrying into the hospital.

The emergency reception desk must have been manned by at least double the normal quota because as soon as Finn came to a halt, someone was asking if they could help.

'I'm Dr Wylie. I was speaking to someone who said they'd arrange a contact with an ambulance dispatcher so we can get around the crash site to our own emergency department at St David's.'

'Just a second, sir,' the young woman said with a courteous smile as she tapped a few buttons to enter the computer system. 'Yes. Here it is. You're to meet up with Charlie outside the door at the end of that corridor. He's going to slot you in between flights carrying fresh supplies to the site, but he said that once he gets you that far you're on your own as far as getting back to St David's.'

'That shouldn't be a problem if they're ferrying as many cases as you are here,' he said grimly. 'Thanks for your help.'

He stepped away from the desk to allow the next in line to take his place and started off down the corridor she'd indicated. As soon as they were away from the frantic hubbub he pulled Freya to the side of the corridor and deposited their bags by her feet.

'If you'd like to take care of these, I'm sure your father will be able to give you a lift home with him at the end of visiting time,' he said hurriedly. 'The police will probably have the road cleared by morning so you could drive my car…'

'What on *earth* are you talking about?' Freya demanded with a glare. 'We've got a flight to catch and we need to do it as soon as possible. There isn't time to go visiting and you needn't think you're leaving me behind.'

'Freya, be sensible. I think it would be much better if you stayed here until tomorrow—'

'*You* think?' she said crossly. 'I wonder what the patients waiting for a doctor would think if they knew I was going to be sitting around chatting when I've got a job to do.'

'Freya, think about it. This is a major incident and it could be hazardous. There's no telling how long you might have to wait for transport out of the danger area.'

'Well, if there *is* any delay, you can be sure I won't be sitting around on my thumbs if there are injured people needing my help,' she said firmly as she bent to grab her bag. 'Anyway, we're wasting time. Or do you want me to carry your bag, too?'

She didn't wait for his reply but set off along the corridor at a smart rate.

Of course he caught her up within a few strides and tried to continue persuading her not to come with him, but once he realised that she wasn't listening he had to be content with muttering something dire under his breath.

Freya had been angry that Finn had thought that she would be happy to sit this emergency out just because it was going to be difficult to get to the hospital. It took a slightly hair-raising trip through the near darkness and a panoramic view of a scene from hell for her to realise that he might genuinely have had her best interests at heart.

The initial point of impact, where the plane had hit the bridge crossing the motorway, was actually a very small part of the area. By far the greater number of casualties were stretched out for almost half a mile in either direction, evidence that the swiftly moving traffic had slewed and crashed in every direction as each had tried to avoid the vehicle in front.

Even though she had just a swift glimpse of the whole scene, already luridly lit by emergency spotlights, she could see that there were an awful lot of them, everything from motorcycles and cars to trucks and lorries. She even spotted what looked like a coach which appeared to have lost control and rolled down an embankment.

Then it all disappeared as the helicopter descended towards the flares that marked its landing area, but the image was burned into Freya's brain and she actually began to wonder if Finn might have been right about this being the wrong place for her to be. After all, there was the safety of the baby to think about now.

It wasn't until the next patient was loaded and the pilot had swiftly departed that Freya could appreciate the strange cacophony that surrounded them.

With normal traffic completely halted in both directions, there was an almost complete absence of moving vehicles. Even the ambulances were using nothing more than their strobe lights as they raced to take yet another victim for further help.

That didn't mean the night was silent, not with dozens of people crying out for help and the pervasive throb of the powerful generators that had been rushed to the site.

'Excuse me, sir, but who are you?' demanded a gruff voice. 'This isn't the time or place for sightseers.'

'I can see that, but it certainly looks as if you could do with some extra pairs of hands,' Finn replied grimly, then introduced himself. The man turned out to be one of the co-ordinators and was quickly able to verify his identity and find out that their hospital was still screaming out for staff.

'Unfortunately, I can't guarantee that I can get you there quickly. It'll depend what sort of injuries we're sending in an ambulance whether there's room for passengers.'

'Would it help if you don't look on us as passengers?' Freya suggested. 'We're quite willing to work our passage.'

'In that case, I've got just the job for you,' he said eagerly. 'We've set up a triage station, but we just can't deal with the basic stuff—like setting up drips and intubating—quickly enough. Once a patient's stabilised we can get them moving, but until then…'

'Well, if you can find somewhere safe for these

bags, we're all yours until you can ship us out,' Finn promised.

He sounded fairly calm, but Freya had caught more than one concerned glance in her direction and suddenly felt guilty. If he was worrying about her, would he be able to keep his mind on what he was doing? She would never forgive herself if she was the reason he wasn't able to do his best for his patients.

Well, it was up to her to put his mind at rest. With all these people around she obviously couldn't do it with words, so it would have to be with her actions. She would be very careful not to put either herself or her baby at risk.

Not that there was much time to think in the next half-hour. The senior site officer hadn't been joking when he'd said they needed help with the sheer volume of basic procedures waiting for them. Freya completely lost track of the number of giving sets she positioned into bloodied, shivering limbs.

'It's almost like being on a production line in a factory,' Finn groaned in an aside that actually raised a smile.

'Who would have thought there would be so many casualties?' Freya added, remembering her shock when she'd learned that there had actually been two coaches involved. One had been out of their sight when they'd approached in the helicopter. It had apparently received relatively little damage, but as the occupants had all been elderly and several had gone into shock they were being put on precautionary IVs. It was always easier to take out a giving set that had proved unnecessary than to try to get one into a vein that had gone flat.

The coach that had rolled down the bank hadn't been so lucky. It had been full of holidaymakers on their way to a two-week whistle-stop tour of Europe, and some of the injuries were far more serious. Two travellers had already been declared dead on site and there were numerous others trapped inside the wreckage.

Freya glanced across at Finn again and caught him looking out across the surrounding carnage towards the sound of heavy lifting and cutting gear in operation. She was almost certain that he would rather be in the thick of things instead of being relegated to relatively minor procedures. But the knowledge that at any moment they could be on their way to the numerous patients lining up for his attention at the hospital seemed to be acting as a brake on his impulse to join in the thick of the action.

She couldn't help a little spurt of selfish relief that he was going to be limited to the relatively safer environment of the accident and emergency department.

There was always a danger in such unstable situations for members of the rescue team to become victims, too. That would be especially true with so many cars around. It wouldn't take more than a spark for any one of them to become an explosive fireball, en-

dangering the lives of everybody in the vicinity. And
with so many damaged vehicles leaking fuel, it could
even set off some sort of chain reaction. With the best
will in the world, the fire crews couldn't isolate every
potential hazard. Some were far too close to victims
who couldn't be moved yet because of the severity
of their injuries.

Although the flood had dwindled to a trickle, there
were still patients waiting for attention before they
could be transferred to one or other of the hospitals.
Nevertheless, neither she nor Finn was sorry when the
time came to be bundled into an ambulance full of
walking wounded.

'Here, hold tight,' Finn murmured as he pulled her
closer, wrapping a strong arm round her to brace her
against the fact that there was very little room on the
last remaining seat. Somehow he'd remembered to
retrieve their bags and had stacked them in the corner
by his ankles.

Freya was almost sitting on his lap but she wasn't
complaining. This might not have been as close as
she'd been hoping they'd get tonight, but it was the
closest they'd been since she'd woken up wrapped
around him like cling film.

There was something infinitely seductive about the
protective way he was holding her, almost as though
she was precious to him. Well, at least daydreaming
was free, she thought with a flash of wry humour,

resisting the sudden urge to snuggle up against him
the way she had on the bench earlier that evening.

It was far more likely that he was concerned that
she should be fit enough to work once they reached
the hospital. Only if she were into self-delusion would
she speculate that he might be regretting the lost
chance to take their tentative flirting to its logical con-
clusion.

'Finn! Where have you been?' demanded the senior
nurse when they finally hurried into the department.
'And Freya! We've been trying to contact you for
hours.'

'Ha! Knowing you doctors, they were probably off
on some secret tryst!' suggested Jonah, one of the
cheekier porters.

'Hardly! They're brother- and sister-in-law, remember,' called Chris Williams.

This time Freya didn't bother to correct him about
their relationship. The junior registrar was looking far
less immaculate than usual and Freya spared a
thought that this major incident would certainly be
make or break for the ambitious young doctor. He
would either decide that this front-line battlefield with
few guarantees of success was what he wanted for his
life, or he would opt for the more serene existence of
ward or theatre work in one of the many other spe-
cialties.

'They're only distant in-laws,' Jonah retorted with

a wicked grin and a wink for the two bags Finn was carrying. 'Nothing 'gainst that if the blood rises hot.'

Freya was hurrying through the department in Finn's long-striding wake, making for the staff lockers and a set of green scrubs, but she felt that blood rising hotly in her face.

Hoping that Jonah wouldn't notice her guilty re-action, she had to put her discomfort to one side. This certainly wasn't the ideal time to defend their honour with the shock announcement of their emergency wedding. Personal matters, including Jonah's wicked teasing, would have to wait until the patients had all been attended to.

After their brief honeymoon would be quite soon enough as far as she was concerned.

When Freya came out in her greens she took an all-encompassing glance around then focused on the board listing both the patients currently under treat-ment and those waiting in cubicles.

'Wow. Is there anyone at home, getting up their strength for tomorrow?' she exclaimed as she joined a senior nurse by the main desk. 'It looks as if almost everyone who works in the department is here and working at full stretch.'

'You could be right, Freya,' she said wearily. 'Are you ready to dive in? I've got about a dozen senior citizens who need your tender touch.'

'I'm ready. Where do you want me to start?' Freya invited.

For almost an hour she worked steadily, doing her best to reassure while she organised for broken bones to be X-rayed and plastered and lacerations to be cleaned and sutured.

There were two patients whose injuries meant they were going to have to undergo hip-replacement surgery. One had actually been delighted because she'd been waiting to go into hospital for just that operation.

Her final patient from the crashed coach was small and slight and had waited uncomplainingly while all her companions were dealt with.

Freya had noticed the way she'd initially had an encouraging word for each as they'd been shown through, but she'd also seen that gradually the woman had become paler.

Now that she was ready to examine the elderly widow fully, she could see the clammy sweat gleaming on her forehead and lip and had an uneasy feeling about her.

'Are you in pain anywhere?' she asked softly as she placed the oxygen mask over her face and attached the ECG monitor. She began a systematic palpation, one eye on the digital readout that was detailing the slow but steady deterioration in her elderly patient's vital signs. Was she going into delayed shock? It certainly wasn't unusual after a traumatic event like this, and especially for someone of her age.

'Well, we did get a bit thrown about when the

coach rolled over,' she said in a noticeably weaker voice all but swamped by the plastic mask.

'Did you hit your head?' Freya asked as she ran her fingers gently through the silvery strands. She couldn't find any evidence of any swelling or ominous dips in the bone, and even though she carefully watched her patient's face she didn't see her wince in pain.

'I don't think so, dear.' The grey-blue eyes were looking slightly confused now, but still very trusting.

'What about your ribs?' Freya used the flat of her palms to check the springing and finally got a reaction when she touched the lowest ribs on the right—a grimace and eyes closed tight against the pressure. 'Is this painful?'

'Not in my ribs exactly. More in my stomach,' she admitted. The fact that she had a protective hand hovering near the area and wasn't even bothering to open her eyes any more was worrying Freya. She'd seemed so alert just a short while ago. Then the patient added, almost too softly to hear over the continuing cacophony outside the cubicle, 'I think I was leaning across to talk to the couple on the other side of the coach when the accident happened. Perhaps the armrest has just bruised me a bit.'

That put a completely different slant on things.

'You don't mind if I take a closer look?' Freya asked urgently, barely waiting long enough for permission before she was signalling for the nurse to help

her dispose of enough clothing to give her an unob-
structed view.

The bruising wasn't obvious at first, but the tension
under the skin told Freya what she needed to know.

'Take 20 mil for a full blood count and rapid cross-
matching, please, get another unit of O running,
quickly and order four more,' she directed while she
reached for the phone. 'We're going to need another
large-bore cannula to push some plasma expander in
if we're going to stand a chance of getting her systolic
blood pressure up to 100,' she warned as she waited
for a connection.

'How soon can I get a patient into surgery?' she
demanded as soon as the phone was answered. 'She's
received blunt trauma at the level of her diaphragm,
resulting in acute haemorrhage.'

'Can you do anything to stabilise her down there?'
asked the voice on the other end. 'We've got patients
queued up for hours.'

'But she can't wait any more,' Freya said force-
fully. In view of the urgency of the situation she was
finding it hard to keep her voice down, but she didn't
want to frighten the stoic little woman. 'She'll bleed
out if we can't stop it soon.'

Finn was rubbing his back muscles as he paced the
length of the corridor, glancing round each curtain.
He was definitely too tall for this job…or everyone
else was too short. At least in Theatre he could have

the specially designed table elevated to a comfortable height. Hours spent bending in concentrated work over a fixed table designed for the 'average' male wasn't doing him any good.

He was just beginning to wonder if Freya had managed to go for a break when he heard her voice. His heart performed a quick somersault in his chest and he was forced to admit that this was the reason he'd been going on his 'tour of inspection'.

It had been too long since he'd last seen her and, like any addiction, he was craving a minute or two with her.

He'd had such plans for tonight. And the way the day had been progressing, from the stolen time spent dangling their feet in the clear stream through their delicious meal to the start of twilight when Freya had willingly sat with her head tucked against him, he'd been certain that she'd be willing to respond to his advances.

Instead, they'd nearly had a stand-up fight when he'd tried to get her to stay safely with her parents instead of taking the flight into such a dangerous zone. He'd lost that fight simply because she'd completely ignored him.

Finn had to admit, in retrospect, that he'd never have managed to cope alone with all the work they'd done while they'd waited for transport to the hospital. On the few occasions when he'd been able to look up from what he'd been doing, he'd been filled with pride at the way she'd calmly and professionally assessed each patient's needs while mayhem had swirled around them. Her skill at inserting IVs swiftly and accurately had been something he'd noticed right from the first day she'd joined his team, as had the sympathetic way she treated her patients. That hadn't changed a bit, even in those trying conditions.

Not that it was Freya's medical skills he was in search of at the moment. It was more a deep need just to see her, with her long dark hair wound up in a hasty knot and the baggy greens hiding the secret that so far only the two of them shared.

Her functional clothing held more than that secret, if his increasingly erotic dreams were to be believed. For months now, he'd had images inside his head of her naked body poised over his or, better yet, under his while he brought them both to ecstasy.

The sound of her voice in something rather less than a loving mood brought him back to his surroundings with a snap.

'She can't wait any more,' he heard her say sharply. 'She'll bleed out if we can't stop it soon.'

He pushed the door open just far enough to stick his head round as she hung up the phone.

'Problem?'

'Yes. Big problem,' she groaned, and he had the feeling that if she hadn't just pulled on a clean pair of gloves she'd have been pulling her hair out. 'This is Mary Swift and she was badly bruised when the coach crashed.'

Finn appreciated the way Freya had stroked the back of her patient's hand when she'd spoken about her. From the weary smile on the little woman's face, she did, too, even though she didn't open her eyes.

Then his own eyes were making a clinical survey of the darkening hue under the tissue-fragile skin, and he knew exactly what Freya was afraid of. His brain was already beginning to tick over faster as he started calculating possibilities.

'I take it you can't get her into Theatre.' It wasn't really a question because he'd overheard her speaking on the phone.

'At least half an hour before there's a chance of it,' she confirmed.

'In that case, it's down to the two of us,' he said, the decision made. 'You've taken blood for a cross-match?'

'Should be back any minute, but I've already got one of O and another of plasma expander both running wide open, and four more of O ready to go. But—' He didn't give her time to question his intentions, even though he knew she wanted to.

'Good girl,' he said, and enjoyed the brief flash of her eyes at the teasing label. 'Let's clear the decks and get on with it. Can you grab someone to do the anaesthetic?'

'With all the theatres going flat out, they're probably scarcer than hen's teeth,' she pointed out, already reaching for the phone.

Finn didn't waste time waiting for the answer, free to busy himself organising the nurses into finding the supplies he needed because he knew Freya wouldn't let him down.

It took nearly ten minutes of telephone bullying and a promise given with her fingers crossed behind her back that the process wouldn't take more than a few minutes, but she found him an anaesthetist.

In the end it took nearly an hour with the two of them working on opposite sides of the table, alternately clearing the operating field of blood and removing or repairing the torn structures.

'What a team,' he said as he left her to do her usual neat line of sutures to close up, then groaned as he straightened up, his back aching worse than ever.

'I keep telling you, you're getting too old for this game,' she said smugly, throwing him a brief glance over her mask out of grey eyes gleaming with pleasure. 'Perhaps you need to think about becoming an anaesthetist, then you could sit down all day.'

'Hey!' Nazim complained from his place at the head of the table where he was gradually lightening the anaesthetic, ready to let their patient wake when the procedure was over. 'Before I agreed to do this I was wonderful Nazim, we can't do without you. Now I'm just the man who sits down all day, doing the easy job.'

Finn laughed aloud. 'Isn't that women for you?' he commiserated. 'All sweetness and light when they want something from you, but then—'

'Can we help it if we're the more pragmatic half of the human race?' Freya said with a look of innocence that belied the gleam in her eyes. 'Sometimes you have to compromise for the sake of the greater good.'

CHAPTER EIGHT

FINN was still thinking about Freya's teasing words when he put his key in the door of his flat later that day.

He'd stopped off to collect the envelope of photos on his way home, reminded of them only when he found the receipt slip in his wallet.

He'd sent Freya home hours ago, not long after Mary Swift had been transferred up to a bed on the surgical ward. That little woman was a tough old bird…a real survivor, not unlike Freya's mother, really. Probably that was one of the reasons Freya had been so determined to save her.

He'd called in on her once she was settled on the ward and had found her already awake and taking intelligent notice of everything going on around her. It had been hard to reconcile the picture with his previous sight of her looking so close to death. She certainly didn't look like someone who'd had her spleen removed and a tear in her diaphragm repaired.

He closed the door behind him and leant back against it with a sigh of relief. He felt so tired that he couldn't even begin to calculate how many hours he'd been awake.

'It's almost as bad as when I was training,' he muttered as he dragged himself upright to remove his jacket and hang it up. His bag felt as if it weighed a ton. 'Actually, everything's worse because I'm ten years older.' Perhaps Freya was right to say he was getting too old. He was thirty-four after all. Was she saying that she thought he was too old to be able to cope with the rigours of a child?

His ego gave him a solid kick. He was only two years younger than Colum, and his brother might complain about Max and Matt but he was obviously enjoying every moment of fatherhood with the five-year-olds. If Colum could do it, so could he.

He'd started to cross his living room when suddenly he stopped in his tracks and sniffed experimentally. Something was different.

He'd been away for a couple of days but the flat certainly didn't have that musty smell it usually had when it had been shut up. In fact, it smelled almost as if someone had been here, cooking.

'Going crazy, too,' he muttered. Senile dementia, perhaps?

The answer to the savoury smell was obvious. Someone in one of the other flats must have been cooking something delicious and the smell had drifted up to linger temptingly in his flat. 'And I probably haven't got anything more than mouldy bread to eat,' he grumbled as his stomach groaned loudly. 'Or the energy to go out and get anything.'

He paused a moment outside the kitchen door and looked down the little hallway towards his bedroom, wondering whether to give up on the idea of eating and opt for a quick shower and a long sleep instead.

His stomach growled again and he sighed as he gave in to the demand and pushed the kitchen door open.

The sight that met him had him staring in amazement. A perfectly arranged place setting awaited him on the little area of work surface that served as a breakfast bar, and in the centre of the placemat…was a note.

'Supper's in the fridge. Microwave two minutes, stir and nuke again. Enjoy. Freya.'

He often saw her neat, very un-doctorly writing in notations on charts, but this was the first time she'd ever written to him. For a moment he actually felt sentimental enough about it to want to keep it, but then his stomach growled again and he opted for practicality.

'Chicken,' he decided when he saw the casserole dish and wondered when she'd had time to make it. 'Probably did it instead of catching up on her sleep,' he muttered crossly while he watched the dish slowly rotate on the turntable. Not that he was cross enough to refuse the meal. He was far too hungry for that.

He was using a soup spoon to scrape up the very last drop of gravy when his thoughts returned to Freya's teasing comment to Nazim.

'Can we help it if we're the more pragmatic half of the human race?' she'd asked. 'Sometimes you have to compromise for the sake of the greater good.'

Was that what had prompted her to accept his offer of marriage? Her innate female pragmatism leading her to accept a possible solution to a known problem, even as her willingness to compromise allowed her to ignore the fact that he wasn't the mate of her choice.

Well, over the last few years he'd heard an awful lot of hype about men getting in touch with their feminine sides. Perhaps this situation was the proof that he had one, too, because he'd been perfectly willing to marry her even though he knew he wasn't her first choice. Pragmatism and compromise in action.

'And when it means I get to come home to meals like that, I'm definitely winning,' he murmured as he got up to wash his plate and cutlery. Now all he needed was enough time when they were both off duty to persuade Freya that theirs was a partnership worth building on.

They were already top-notch when it came to working together in the accident and emergency department. It had been almost uncanny when they'd stationed themselves on either side of Mary Swift. Not once had either of them got in the other's way. They'd barely needed to speak to each other, both knowing what needed to be done and the best way to achieve it.

Unfortunately, Finn's dreams were telling him that

it would be every bit as good when they finally made love—both in tune with each other, knowing exactly what to do to give each other pleasure...

'Enough!' he groaned as he retrieved his wash-kit and went into the bathroom on dragging feet. He was tired enough to sleep standing up. The last thing he needed was to be so aroused that it kept him awake for hours, and if he started reliving those dreams...

It must have been one of the shortest showers on record, and he did little more than drag a towel over his body before he made for the bedroom, roughly drying his hair as he went.

He was actually standing right beside the bed before he realised that there was already someone sleeping in it.

'Freya,' he breathed, his heart starting to thump unevenly as he took in the sight of her dark hair spread out across the pillow. It was just like the images in his dreams, only this time it was actually happening. She was actually here, curled up so that she faced the empty pillow where his head would lie, with one hand reaching across as though searching for him.

To say he was amazed to see her there was an understatement. He didn't know why, tiredness probably, but when she'd said she was going home, he'd thought she'd meant she was going back to her little top-floor flat.

He'd actually managed to forget that he was married, so finding her there amazed him, but it also delighted him more than he'd be able to express.

It was just a relief that she hadn't been awake when he'd walked in through the door or she'd have seen him standing there gaping down at her like someone with a few marbles loose.

And if she woke up now, she'd have indisputable proof of just how pleased he was to have her in his bed, lying there like some sleeping princess.

For another moment he stood there, drinking in the sight of her, then he gently eased back the covers and slid under to join her.

She stirred and he held his breath, not really certain whether he was hoping she would awake or stay asleep. He realised that they were legally married and that she'd willingly shared his bed at the hotel, but this was his home turf and until he'd had a chance to talk to her he wasn't sure what the rules were.

He'd actually been cowardly enough not to mention it before the wedding, superstitious that it might stop the ceremony going ahead.

He knew what he was hoping…that she really had been just as eagerly looking forward to sharing their honeymoon bed that second night as he had. For the moment he was going to have to compose his soul in patience and try to be satisfied with the fact that she'd obviously accepted his flat as their home. If they were going to be sharing the same bed night after night, surely that must increase his chances of finding out whether his dreams really could come true.

With his head pillowed on one arm he lay facing her and drank in the elfin perfection of her face, suddenly filled with the fervent hope that the child she carried would resemble her and not the faceless man who'd fathered it.

Because the baby was hers he knew it was going to be easy to love him or her, but it would be easier to forget that he hadn't been there for that precious moment of conception if the child took after her side of the family.

Still, he may not have been there when this child had been conceived, but if everything went the way he hoped it would, he'd definitely be there for the next one.

He closed his eyes and stifled a groan when his body reacted all too predictably. It was obviously far too long since he'd had anything but self-administered relief, and once Freya had come to join his team at the hospital, even that had become unacceptable.

Drawing in a deep breath and sending up a fervent prayer for patience and endurance, he deliberately shut his thoughts down, the way he'd learned to do during his training when every minute of slumber had been essential, and slid into sleep.

Freya didn't need to open her eyes to know that Finn was in bed beside her. It was blatantly obvious when she was once more wrapped around him almost as closely as his own skin.

She stifled a groan when she remembered that she'd intended waiting up for him to ask if he'd actually intended for the two of them to share his flat. She knew it was a stupid point and he'd never said anything either way, but she'd been afraid he might think she was being presumptuous. Except this marriage had been his idea and he'd been adamant that he was in it for the long haul.

The trouble was, she needed her sleep these days, almost as much as she had during the endless duties when she'd been training, and his bed had looked so comfortable that she'd given in and curled up in it.

Even then, she'd thought she would hear him when he finally returned home, certain that the sound of his meal preparations in the kitchen would wake her even if the key in the front door didn't.

Obviously pregnancy was making her sleep more heavily, or perhaps it was the fact that she'd been working at full stretch for several very intense hours without so much as a bathroom break that had exhausted her.

Whatever it was, she was now in exactly the same embarrassing position she'd found herself in the other morning, with her head pillowed on Finn's shoulder, her arm across his chest and her leg... Oh, please, not again, she groaned silently. It had been bad enough the first time. Didn't the man ever wake up without such fervent proof that he was healthy and happy to have female company? This time was even worse because the door was on the other side of the bed. If she was going to make a run for sanctuary, she was going to have to gallop around the bed to do it.

'Did you ever see that film *Groundhog Day*?' demanded an all-too-familiar morning-husky voice.

'I don't think so. What's it about?'

'The people in it are condemned to repeat the same day over and over again until they get it right.'

'Oh.' She nearly choked on her embarrassment.

She'd thought the unexpected line of conversation was a way of saving her face again, but instead he'd chosen to confront the situation. Surely she'd known him long enough to be able to predict that he'd do that. It wasn't really his way to pussyfoot about.

'The only thing is,' he continued, his voice filling the breadth and depth of the chest under her ear, 'it takes the hero an awful long time of trial and error before he discovers what is the right way, and I'd rather not waste time.'

'Oh,' she said again nervously, uncertain where this was going. It wasn't until she realised that his pulse had picked up and that his breathing was noticeably faster that she realised he wasn't nearly as calm as he appeared.

'So, do you want some help moving the rest of

your things over here, or did you just stay for one night because you were too tired to go to your flat after you'd cooked that delicious meal?'

Freya couldn't help the chuckle that escaped.

'Trust you to make any question so convoluted that I haven't got a clue how to answer it in less than three volumes,' she complained.

'How about a précis of volume one, then. Just give me the gist of it,' he suggested, his own tone notice-ably more relaxed since he'd made her laugh. Still, she didn't quite have the courage to meet those dev-astating green eyes. Not until she'd got the worst of it over with and heard his reaction. He could be upset at her presumption, especially as she seemed totally unable to stay on her side of the bed.

'Well, I thought that since our parents saw us get married, they would expect us to be living together. And as you're about fifteen feet tall and my bed is less than a quarter of that, you'd be more comfortable if I moved in here.'

He was silent for so long that she wondered if he was ever going to speak. In the end she couldn't stand the suspense and turned her head just enough to look up at him.

She wasn't sure what she saw in his face. It was certainly an expression she'd never seen before and one that made her own heartbeat more than a little ragged.

'Hmm,' he said as though coming to some sort of

decision, but she could tell from the wicked glint in his eyes that he'd found a light-hearted way to cover up what he was really thinking. 'Does that mean that, as I'm providing the roof over your head, you'll be doing all the cooking?'

'In your dreams,' she scoffed, and was seared by a sudden flash of heat in his eyes.

He must have seen her startled reaction because the flames were doused as quickly as they had appeared.

'Well, at least I'll be able to dream about that chicken casserole,' he mused in resigned tones. 'You'll never know how welcome that was when I came in at stupid-o'clock this morning.'

'I didn't even hear you,' she admitted. 'What time did you come in? You're not on early duty this morning, are you?'

'No, thank goodness. I can actually enjoy the luxury of a lie-in…or I could have if someone hadn't woken me up.' He glanced meaningfully at the arm still draped across his chest and Freya suddenly realised to her horror that her leg was *still* nestled in its embarrassing position.

'Well, I'm sorry if I woke you,' she began, only to stop when she felt a strange sensation deep inside.

She held her breath for several seconds and waited hopefully. She'd been feeling the odd flutter for several weeks, now that the baby was growing bigger and stronger, but nothing as strong as that before.

She'd almost given up when it happened again.

'Finn,' she squeaked, almost breathless with excitement as she finally smiled up into his eyes. 'Did you feel that?'

'Feel what?' He looked startled and she suddenly realised that he might have thought she was referring to his own physical reaction to her proximity.

Eager for him to share the miracle going on inside her, she quickly rolled onto her back, grabbing his hand to press it to the gentle curve of her belly where the activity seemed to be centred.

'Wait a minute and it might happen again,' she gabbled. 'It's been going on for several weeks now and getting stronger all the time.'

If Finn was disconcerted at having his hand grabbed and unceremoniously plastered against her naked stomach, he didn't have time to complain because almost as soon as she'd placed it there she felt a definite thump.

'There! Did you feel it?' she crowed.

'Good God!' he exclaimed, snatching his hand away and staring down at her as though unable to believe what was going on. 'Did that hurt?'

'Not at all, so far. It just feels a little…weird. Like unexpectedly lively indigestion.'

She could almost see the thoughts running through his head as he stared down at the curve that, thanks to a deceptively spacious pelvis, was still barely there in spite of the fact that she was already halfway through the pregnancy.

She was watching as consternation mixed with awe then finally gave way to something much darker that looked almost like anger as he finally snatched his hand away.

Disappointment speared through her as he rolled away without another word. For a second he sat on the edge of the bed without moving and she wondered if he was actually going to say something. Then, with a muttered imprecation, he strode out of the room completely naked and she realised that he'd only been angry that there was nothing to hand to cover himself.

Not that she was sorry.

The way things were going at the moment, the occasional glimpse of those world-class buns was about as good as her marriage was going to get.

'Nonsense!' she hissed decisively as she reached for the silky wrap Astrid had brought back for her from her honeymoon.

She was married to Finn, for better or for worse, and if it was going to be up to her to make sure that it was better rather than worse, then it was time she started putting a bit of effort into it.

By the time the shower stopped and Finn emerged from the bathroom, the flat was full of the enticing scent of freshly brewed coffee and grilling bacon.

She was wearing a welcoming smile as he came into the kitchen, and when she saw the startled expression on his face it just grew wider.

'I presume you don't eat cereal as there wasn't any

in the cupboard,' she said brightly as she poured orange juice into the two glasses she'd set out on the breakfast bar. There hadn't been much time to set things out prettily, but once she got the hang of this 'wifely' stuff…

It wasn't as if this was really a new scenario. It just happened to have been one of her fondest dreams ever since she'd met the man. And now she had the chance to live it, she wasn't going to let it slip away.

'Actually, there wasn't much of anything,' she continued, beckoning him over, 'so I had to drive out last night to the all-night shop at the end of the high street to stock up a bit. Do you want marmalade with your toast?'

She was tempted to giggle when she saw how shell-shocked he looked. This obviously hadn't been the reception he'd expected after he'd disappeared into the bathroom like that, and although he probably wasn't aware how much his face was giving away, he was equally obviously delighted.

In complete silence he took his place on one of the stools and watched as she took the other, bringing with her the plate of grilled bacon and tomatoes.

'Uh, Freya…' he began warily, but she was on a roll and wasn't about to let him interrupt.

'I know this is a bit of a luxury, to sit down to breakfast together. When our shifts are at odds with each other we might not do much more than pass each other on the road between here and the hospital, but I thought we might as well start off on the right foot.'

Her hands were working just as efficiently as her tongue, setting an appetising array of piping hot food in front of him, as well as a plate of toast and a cup of coffee, and all without him getting a word in edgeways.

'I'm due on duty before you today,' she continued between bites, surreptitiously monitoring Finn's expression as he filled his fork for the first time then hiding a relieved smile when he quickly came back for another mouthful. 'So, I thought that you could do the washing-up for me while I get dressed. Perhaps we could alternate or something, to keep it fair. And as for supper tonight—'

'Freya...' he interrupted with a chuckle, just before she ran out of things to say without sounding like a broken record. 'Relax, please, or we're both going to end up with indigestion.'

She finally dared to meet his eyes and had to hide a huge sigh of relief when she saw the wicked gleam in those beautiful green eyes. She'd probably overplayed her hand dreadfully, but it didn't seem to have done any harm. In fact, Finn seemed particularly pleased with himself as he grinned around an enormous bite of perfectly browned toast.

So, she thought a short while later as she set off for the hospital, the rocky start seemed to have been smoothed over.

At the time she hadn't understood the strange mood that had sent him stalking naked across the room but, now that she'd had time to think about it, it must have been that same thorn in Finn's side—the fact that he didn't know who had fathered her child.

Ever since she'd realised that he was suffering from drug-induced amnesia she'd been wondering if there was anything that could be done to recover it. None of the books she'd glanced through last night, and Finn had a fair selection of them in the small study at the end of the hallway, had been of any help. Perhaps she should have a word with an anaesthetist, or even a psychologist.

If there was no way of jogging his memory she was just going to have to hope that she could convince him that her version of events on that fateful trip was the truth.

Finn poured the last of the coffee into his cup and carried it through to the sitting room to sit in his favourite chair.

He could still feel that smug smile spread all over his face when he remembered the sight of Freya, his fiercely independent, often fiery, endlessly sexy Freya, standing there in his kitchen, trying to pretend that she'd always been the perfect housewife.

Not that he hadn't appreciated her efforts. He had, enormously. He couldn't remember the last time a woman had cooked breakfast for him, unless it had been his mother and that had been before he'd left home to begin his medical training.

The fact that Freya had gone to so much trouble had touched him profoundly and had raised all those hopes again. The hopes that, even though their marriage had been an emergency gesture to ease her mother's mind, it could eventually become everything he'd ever dreamed it could be.

Finn closed his eyes and leant his head back against the chair, picturing again the long dark spirals of Freya's hair spread across her shoulder and his chest. Just the thought of it made him ache with the need to find out if it was as soft and silky as it looked. And as for her skin…this morning she'd actually taken his hand in hers and placed it on her body.

For one glorious second he'd actually thought she'd been inviting him to touch her all over, and the shock had been so overwhelming that he'd been afraid he was going to disgrace himself. Then he'd realised that she'd placed his hand over the gentle curve of her belly, where her baby was growing.

The unexpectedly sharp movement under his palm had made him freeze in disbelief. For some reason he hadn't expected to be able to feel the tiny limbs moving, and the indisputable proof that there was a real little person alive in there had crashed over him with the power of a tsunami.

He'd felt awed and humbled by the miracle of it, and then desperately, bitterly jealous that he hadn't been the one to put it there, that he was feeling another man's child moving inside the woman he loved.

He was being torn apart inside, one part of him already protective of both mother and baby, the other wanting to demand why she hadn't chosen him to father it when he was the one who'd loved her for so long.

He was honest enough to know that at some stage he was going to have to ask her, but he was wise enough to know that it wasn't something he could just blurt out.

He'd taken a chance when he'd offered to marry her. Only *he* knew that, in effect, he'd been laying his heart in front of her in the hope that one day she'd return his love.

Now he was going to have to be patient. He was going to have to bide his time until she trusted him enough to speak about the man who'd held her heart in his hand and had trampled on it, denying their child a father.

He took a mouthful of coffee and grimaced when he found it had gone cold. A glance at his watch told him it wasn't worth making another pot. He was going to have to report for work in less than an hour and there was the kitchen to tidy yet.

He was grinning again as he got out of his chair, remembering the way Freya had tried to organise an informal schedule to divide up the household duties, and caught sight of the envelope of photos he'd brought home with him the previous night.

He toyed for a minute with the idea of looking at them with Freya when they both returned home later, but couldn't resist a sneak preview.

'Not bad,' he murmured when he saw the way Tom Bishop had managed to take so many shots that captured the informal mood of such an essentially formal occasion. The man obviously had a real gift for photography, and he had every intention of telling him so.

There were several group pictures, each with different members of the family caught together. He couldn't help smiling at the one of Colum and himself laughing and just knew that had been taken when his brother had been warning him he was going to embarrass everyone if he carried on kissing Freya like that.

There was a lovely one of Astrid and Freya together, their arms around each other. How the man had managed not to show Astrid crying was a minor miracle in itself.

Then there was one of Colum and Freya smiling at each other, as though they'd just shared some secret...

Suddenly the world ground to a halt as his heart stopped beating, his gaze going frantically from Freya's wide grey eyes to his brother's hazel ones, and all he could remember was the day he'd been introduced to his brother's new girlfriend.

'I think she might be the one,' Colum had said when he'd invited Finn to join them for a meal, two brothers with two sisters. Finn could remember teasing him about volunteering to put his head in the marital noose but he'd cared enough about his brother to agree to make up the foursome. He'd even been a little intrigued to find out what sort of woman had changed perennially popular Colum so that he'd been willing to embrace monogamy.

Then he'd seen the loving expression on Freya's face when she'd looked up at handsome big brother Colum, and for the first time in his life he'd realised that it was possible to hate someone and love them at the same time.

In that split second he'd realised that, for good or ill, he'd lost his heart for ever to an elfin live wire, and that meant that he and Colum would forever be adversaries.

It had only been a minor reprieve from his continuing misery when Astrid and Colum had been so smitten with each other, but it certainly hadn't lessened his own misery.

Until Freya had confessed her predicament and he'd deliberately engineered the solution that came closest to fulfilling all his hopes.

Just staring at that photo of Colum and Freya was

a stark reminder that things rarely turned out the way he expected.

Over the last six years he'd grown close to Colum again, close enough to want him present on the day that Freya married him. But right at this very moment, looking at the shared expression caught by the camera, he was almost afraid that he was capable of murder, because it looked as if Freya was still in love with Colum.

He felt sick enough to lose every mouthful of that delicious breakfast because if that was true, there a possibility that Colum had fathered her baby.

CHAPTER NINE

FREYA had been so tempted that even now, hours later, she knew it was only the expression on Finn's face that helped her to resist.

They'd only been apart for a few hours, for heaven's sake. Hours in which, when she wasn't being the best emergency physician she could be, her thoughts had ranged over all the possible avenues her campaign to win Finn's heart could take.

Then she'd emerged from behind the cubicle curtain, after removing yet another foreign object from yet another childish nose, and there he'd been, as large as life and twice as enticing.

She'd known that she'd been staring at him, her eyes greedily devouring every inch of that tall muscular frame, but she hadn't been able to drag them away. What she'd really wanted had been to be able to throw herself into his arms and lose herself in a kiss just like the one they'd shared in the hospital chapel.

She couldn't guarantee that she'd want to stop with a kiss, not if its effect on her was as potent as the last one, and this was hardly the place to start something they couldn't finish. But, still, she was tempted...

Then she realised that he wasn't smiling and that the expression in those changeable green eyes was chilly...almost accusatory... Finn was definitely not in the mood for any sort of seduction.

Or was she misreading the signs? Was there something else on his mind entirely?

'Oh, God!' Immediately her thoughts flew to her mother. 'Finn? What's happened? Is it Mum?'

She almost heard the gears change inside his head as he gave a startled blink.

'I haven't heard anything since you last spoke to them,' he said decisively.

'But...the expression on your face...' Her heart was still pounding, hardly daring to believe that all was well.

'I was just...' He hesitated, and that was unusual in itself. Then he seemed to come to some sort of decision. 'I was thinking about something else entirely, Freya. Something that we need to talk about.'

'Now?' Her pulse had just begun to slow but it was thudding uncomfortably again now. 'Is it hospital business? Should we go to your office?'

There was that flash of indecision again and tension began to coil tightly inside her, bringing with it an inexplicable dread.

He shook his head, the clinically bright light above him striking red and gold gleams in his tawny hair. 'Tonight will do. When we get home,' he said, but he didn't look happy.

She worried at the conversation for several hours, like a terrier with a bone, trying to come up with a topic that would make Finn look so sombre.

Knowing that her mother was progressing well—a quick phone call had been enough to settle her worries on that score—and given that he'd implied that the topic was nothing connected with the hospital, she was at a loss.

Unless…

Unless it was something to do with their marriage?

But even that didn't hold water. They'd both gone into the marriage for pragmatic reasons and the fact that she'd been in love with the man for years had no bearing on the situation…unless she'd given away the fact that she loved him.

But would that make any difference?

He'd said when he'd first put forward the idea that it was up to the two of them to make theirs a good partnership. He'd also brought up the fact that Ruth was as vehemently against divorce as she was illegitimacy, so he surely couldn't be going to suggest ending their pact just because she was in love with him.

But if it wasn't that, what could it be? All she knew was that it was something that made him look unhappy.

He looked even unhappier when Chris Williams cornered him in the staffroom. Chris was obviously oblivious of Freya's presence in the corner by the post rack when he asked Finn if he had any tips to persuade Freya to go out with him.

Hardly able to believe her ears, her gaze flew across the room to meet the hard malachite eyes waiting for her.

Wordlessly she shook her head, hoping Finn would understand it as a signal that she'd never encouraged the younger man's interest.

His brief nod seemed to accept the assurance.

'Chris, I think you're going to have to accept that you're on a hiding to nothing with Freya,' he advised gently.

'Why? You don't think she fancies me?'

Freya couldn't hide her grin at his youthful arrogance in his own attractiveness to the opposite sex. Apparently it was inconceivable to him that anyone would turn him down if he just found the right approach.

Perhaps he was right if the woman in question wasn't already in love with someone else.

'Actually, I think it's more a case of knowing that her attentions are focused in another direction,' Finn said carefully, in an echo of her own thoughts, had he but known it.

This time when he glanced across at her Freya saw a glint of humour lightening the colour of his eyes and softening them.

'Another direction? Who?' Chris demanded persistently, almost indignantly. 'The only person who gets more than a cheerful smile as they get the brush-off is you, and you're already related to her, well, almost.'

'That does mean that I'm privy to information the rest of you don't have,' Finn pointed out with what sounded like a deliberate touch of mystery. He'd obviously given up correcting the younger man's assumptions, too. 'I'll give you a little clue, Chris. Take a look at her ring finger.'

He left Chris spluttering in his wake, clearly desperate for more details that, for Freya's immediate peace of mind, weren't forthcoming.

She stayed still and quiet in her corner until Chris left the room then blew out a resigned breath.

She'd been enjoying this secret interlude where, in the whole of St David's, only she and Finn knew what they'd done. She'd always known that they wouldn't be able to keep their marriage quiet for long—keeping it a secret would actually be defeating the whole object—and she'd been dreading the third-degree they'd doubtless get from their colleagues, but there was no alternative, especially as her pregnancy grew more advanced.

Even if they didn't make a general announcement, the hospital accounts department would have to be notified soon so that they could change her details for tax and benefit purposes. Once that was done, the highly efficient grapevine would spread the news far and wide.

In the meantime, the fact that she now wore a wedding ring was camouflaged for almost the whole of the rest of her shift as she donned pair after pair of disposable gloves to deal with bodily fluids of every description.

Her final patient of the day was easily the most shocking, a young man who'd been setting out in high spirits to celebrate his eighteenth birthday. Almost before he'd had a chance to sample his first pint he'd fallen foul of a neighbourhood bully who, without blinking an eye, had taken out a switchblade and slashed it across the teenager's throat.

'What's your name?' she asked clearly, as she leant over him to peer under the latest wad of rapidly darkening dressing he was holding against the gaping wound. She'd found that starting with a simple question often made more complicated ones easier to tackle for a frightened patient.

'John,' he managed in a terrified rasp with both hands pressing the dressing against his throat. 'John Thatcher.'

'Well, John, I'm Freya and I'm a doctor,' she said, hoping he couldn't see her shock at the severity of the injury. 'Can you tell me how long ago you last had anything to eat?'

'Can't you see it through the hole?' he demanded shakily with a parody of humour that made Freya give a startled laugh.

'You're obviously a survivor if you've got a sense of humour like that,' she said as her grin lingered.

'So I'm not going to die?'

There was the vulnerability she'd expected in a young man who was suddenly facing the prospect of imminent death when he'd thought he had his whole life ahead of him.

'Not on *my* watch, as they say in all the best action films,' she quipped. 'The paramedics have already got you hooked up to fluids to replace what you've lost, and I'm sending for a specialist to check any damage to the tissues inside your throat.'

She kept her tone even and friendly because it was important to calm him down if she could. A slow heartbeat would make him lose less blood than one that was racing. There was no point in telling him that it looked as if his assailant had nicked his jugular vein. At least it hadn't been the carotid artery or there would have been a high-pressure scarlet fountain erupting out of his throat.

As it was, it sounded as if his voice had escaped injury and as his breathing didn't seem compromised his trachea was still intact, but there were several muscles that were going to need careful piecing together, as well as the long ugly gash in his skin.

'Will you be stitching me up?' he demanded, obviously calmer now, but whether that was down to her bedside manner or the pain relief he'd been given was a moot point.

'I don't know yet. We'll have to wait until the specialist's seen you. You could even get the five-star treatment and be taken up to Theatre.'

She'd nearly rolled her eyes when she recognised the dawning admiration in his eyes. The last thing she needed was hero-worship from someone more than ten years younger than herself. Finn was the only one she wanted to fall in love with her.

'Speaking purely of the tissue damage,' the specialist pronounced plummily a short while later, 'the blade must have been very sharp because it delivered a very clean cut. The severed ends should go together well. Just make sure you irrigate sufficiently in case the weapon was still contaminated by residue from previous victims.'

Freya thanked him gravely for his time then signalled for a suture tray as soon as he waddled his self-important way along the corridor.

The repair was a slow, painstaking job, hampered at first by the amount of blood continually flooding the area. Only when she'd inserted the tiny stitches to close the nick in the jugular did things become easier, but it was still more than an hour and a half before she finally straightened up.

'There you are. All done,' she announced as she stripped off yet another set of blood-stained disposable gloves and dropped them in the bin. 'I'm afraid you'll never be perfect again, John, but you'll definitely have a scar worth showing to your girlfriends.'

With a promise that she would have a word with his parents before sending them up to join him for the start of his overnight stay on the ward and also ask the police who were waiting to talk to him to come back tomorrow, she backed out through the swinging door of the trauma room and crashed straight into Finn.

'You were supposed to go off duty nearly an hour ago,' he accused with a frowning glance at his watch.

'Well...' She shrugged. 'You know how it is when you're enjoying yourself. I just couldn't bring myself to leave a young man to bleed to death on his birthday.'

'Smart alec,' he muttered with a scowl that couldn't have intimidated her if it had tried. 'You could have asked someone to take over. You shouldn't be exhausting yourself, especially since the major incident the other night.'

'It wasn't a problem, Finn,' she reassured him, a warm glow spreading through her at the evidence of his concern. Perhaps she'd been wrong to worry about the talk he wanted to have tonight. 'I've only been sitting down doing some embroidery for the last hour and a half. Actually, it was an interesting case. An eighteen-year-old had his throat cut with a switchblade.'

'What?'

That had caught his attention, and all the way to the lockers she regaled him with the specifics of the injuries inflicted and how she'd had to repair them. He'd retaliated with the gruesome details of the patient who'd shot himself in the foot with a nail gun and had arrived at the hospital with a length of timber still attached to his foot.

She mentally replayed the conversation later as she was sprinkling grated cheese over a dish of macaroni cheese, ready to brown under the grill, and started chuckling at the incongruity.

There couldn't be many newly-weds who would revel in such gory sweet talk. What a good job it was that the two of them had so much in common. She would have been frustrated not to have been able to share the complexities of her job with someone who understood what she'd achieved.

At the same time, there would be few who didn't work in the high-pressure world of a hospital who would even *see* the dark humour in some of the grisly situations they saw on a daily basis.

She'd made a mixed leaf salad to go with the macaroni and set the fruit bowl nearby ready for dessert before she realised how time was slipping away.

Finn was going to be arriving soon and she wanted to have a shower and change into something fresh before she had to face him this evening. It might only be a surface thing and only she would know that she'd gone to so much trouble, but it would give her that little extra bit of confidence to know she was looking her casual best.

A pair of silky trousers—with a drawstring waist, of course, she decided with a grimace, now that the child inside her was beginning to be a visible presence. She would have liked to have worn a skimpy vest top in honour of the lingering warmth of the summer day, instead of the cream silk tunic. Unfortunately, when she'd tried it on she'd realised that she probably wasn't going to be able to wear it again… unless she lost the extra inches that had begun to swell the once meagre curves of her bust.

'Still, it's quite nice to be able to look down and see a decent cleavage for a change…or should that be an indecent cleavage?' she mused aloud with a grin as she dropped her discarded clothes into the laundry basket and stepped naked into the shower.

She stood to one side and was just adjusting the temperature of the spray before stepping under it when she caught sight of something out of the corner of her eye.

With a shriek she ducked through the water and charged out of the cubicle, leaving it to the biggest, hairiest spider she'd ever seen in her life.

Before she had a chance to decide what she was going to do about it, or even think about wrapping a towel around herself, the bathroom door flew open and Finn charged in.

'What happened, Freya?' he demanded urgently, her shriek still echoing in his ears. 'Did you hurt…?'

His words caught in his throat and nearly strangled

him when he saw her standing there, totally naked and dripping wet.

The shower was still running behind her but it was the droplets running down her face and over her body that riveted his attention.

It was his most erotic dream come to life in front of his eyes, and for a moment he wasn't sure whether he was dreaming again or whether he'd died and gone to heaven.

'Finn!' she squeaked, apparently oblivious of her nakedness as she whirled away from him to point. 'It's in there and it's *enormous*!'

He blinked as reality and dreams diverged.

In his dream she'd stared at him because he'd been all but naked, too, and they'd been drawn together as though magnetically attracted.

In reality she'd barely given him a second glance, clad as he was in the shirt and trousers he'd worn to go to the hospital that morning. All she'd been interested in had been pointing to something in the shower.

He took a couple of wary steps towards her then, when he realised he was courting heart failure the closer he got, grabbed a towel from the rail and draped it around her.

'Here. You'll get chilled,' he said, completely ignoring the fact that it was midsummer and the bathroom was filling with warm steam from the shower.

'Thanks,' she said distractedly as she peered with

awful fascination into the cubicle. 'Can you get it out?'

'What?' She obviously wasn't thinking what she was saying or she'd have phrased her request differently, or was that the hormone-crazed teenager hidden inside him talking?

'*That*,' she said with utter loathing. 'I can't stand them, especially when they're large enough to feed a family of four.'

Finn finally caught sight of the spider cowering in the corner and had to fight an urge to laugh aloud. He'd expected to see something the size of a tarantula at least, not this common or garden house spider.

Without a word he reached in and turned off the water then grabbed an apricot-coloured tissue from the box which had mysteriously appeared beside the basin.

Within seconds he'd liberated Freya's nemesis out of the window and dropped the tissue in the toilet, then he had to perform the more difficult task—to turn and face Freya, knowing that she was standing there without a stitch on under that loosely draped towel.

He steeled himself and swung around to find a pair of wide grey eyes fixed on him as though he'd performed a heroic deed on a par with St George fighting the fire-breathing dragon.

The expression was good for his ego but hell on his self-control.

'Uh…were you nearly finished with the shower?' He groaned silently when he realised that he was almost reduced to stammering by the sight of this half-pint sprite. 'Will there be time for me to take one before we eat?'

'No. Yes. I mean…' She shook her head distractedly.

He barely noticed her garbled answer. All he was conscious of was the way *his* body was reacting to the way *her* eyes were skating over it, almost…almost as if she was imagining him stripping off to take his shower.

For just a moment he contemplated doing just that, suggesting that they share the shower, perhaps, in the interests of saving water and preserving the planet's precious resources.

The expression in Freya's eyes as she looked at him and the way she'd trapped just the tip of her tongue between her teeth nearly had steam coming out of his ears. He was a hair's breadth away from reaching for the first button when he remembered why he'd come home early tonight, and all thoughts of seduction fled.

Finn didn't know what she saw when she finally met his eyes but it snapped her out of her languid perusal.

'Um, no, Finn. I'd only just started the water running when I saw *that* in there with me.' She gestured towards the window with a shudder. 'But there'll be plenty of time for both of us to shower. The food just needs putting under the grill when we're ready for it.'

He stifled a groan as he left the bathroom, wondering if he'd just blown his best chance for taking their relationship that crucial step towards real intimacy.

Logically, he knew that he would never be satisfied with just a sexual relationship. Without being bigheaded, he knew he'd had had plenty of opportunities over the last few years, but once his heart had decided on Freya, nothing and no one else would have done.

The trouble was, as far as he knew, his situation hadn't changed from where it had been the first day he'd met Freya. He was in love with her and she was in love with Colum.

One part of his brain was trying to persuade him that he should be seizing his chance to show Freya that hankering after Colum was a mistake. It was telling him that he should be putting his efforts into persuading her to take advantage of their new situation, to make a completely different life for herself.

The other part was far less opportunistic, knowing that a wrong step this early on could lead to massive heartbreak further down the road.

It was one thing to love the woman and be willing to commit himself to her and her unborn child for a lifetime, but he needed to be able to hope that she would eventually come to love him, too. It would be another thing entirely to bare his heart to her, only to find out that she still loved Colum too much to ever contemplate loving another man.

Freya stood under the shower with her face tipped up into the full force of the water and groaned with a mixture of embarrassment and frustration.

She would never forget the way shock had widened Finn's moss green eyes in those first startled seconds. Neither could she forget the last time she'd seen it happen, nearly five months ago.

It had been her first conference abroad since she'd moved to the same accident and emergency department as Finn—just two days away from the hospital in the breathtaking surroundings of central Paris—and Finn had been presenting a short paper.

The whole conference had been hard work for her because she'd conscientiously attended every lecture and presentation and taken sheaves of notes, but she'd also thoroughly enjoyed the chance of going out with a multinational group of delegates to visit some of the sights synonymous with Paris.

Finn had been part of the group and, as he'd been to Paris before, had acted as their unofficial tour guide.

They'd made a whistle-stop visit to the Louvre on the first evening, taking advantage of the extended closing time, and Freya had insisted on catching a quick glimpse of the Mona Lisa. The second day they'd woven their way through the lunchtime crowds around the Eiffel Tower and the Arc de Triomphe.

At the end of the conference there was just an hour free before they needed to set off for the airport. The rest of the group had decided that it was too damp and cold to do anything other than sit in a café, but Freya was determined to drink real French coffee while watching the Seine flow by.

Finn groaned theatrically but was the only one to bring his steaming drink out to join her as she leaned against the balustraded wall to stare down into the water.

They didn't say much but, with all of historic Paris spread out around them, words weren't really needed. It was enough that she was in one of the most romantic cities in the world with Finn at her side.

It was one of those perfect moments that she was sure she would remember all her life. It didn't matter that within minutes they were surrounded by their colleagues again, reminding them that it was time to leave. For just those few moments life was perfect.

Then it was time to return to England, with Max's and Matt's fifth birthday party just hours away, and Charles de Gaulle airport had been closed by fog.

Officials kept reassuring them that all would be well, that it would just take a little longer than expected before they could depart. But, they shrugged, where was the problem in spending a few more hours with a beautiful woman in the most romantic city in the world?

Finn didn't bother trying to explain that the two of them were expected to arrive in England in time to watch two little boys blow out their candles. The weather wasn't going to be paying any attention to their needs.

The offer of a lift to Calais for the British contingent seemed like the answer to a prayer to Freya. Phone calls had failed to find seats on the Shuttle under the Channel, but there would be no problem getting a crossing on the ferry. With a fast rail link from Dover to London they could probably still make the end of the party by the skin of their teeth.

Finn had seemed uneasy with the arrangements and for five months Freya had thought it had been because he'd been concerned about letting their nephews down. It was only *now* that she knew it had been his debilitating seasickness that had concerned him.

She wrapped a towel around her hair like a turban and pulled a wry face at herself in the mirror.

It had only been after the event that she'd realised just how closely the incident this evening had echoed the situation on the ferry. It had been a spider which had caused her to shriek today—on the crossing, it had been a deluge of icy water when she'd expected warm.

She shivered at the recollected shock and suddenly

remembered that while she was in here rehashing history, Finn was waiting for his turn under the shower.

If she'd been a little bolder or a little quicker to react, would she have been able to tempt him into sharing the shower with her? She was going to need to be a whole lot faster on the uptake if she was going to succeed as a seductress.

Too late now. There was a meal to eat and a serious conversation of some sort waiting for her before she could get on with her plans to seduce him.

But then, watch out, Finn. Freya Innes…no, Freya *Wylie* was out to get her man.

CHAPTER TEN

FINN was obviously preoccupied and the way he was playing with his food, instead of eating it, was putting Freya off her meal, too.

'Oh, for heaven's sake!' she exclaimed as she dumped her cutlery impatiently on her plate, suddenly fed up with the suspense. 'Can we, *please*, get this conversation over with so we can get on with our lives?'

She'd thought his expression had been grim before, but by the time she'd led the way into the sitting room and thumped down inelegantly into one corner of the settee, it was downright forbidding.

For a moment it looked as though he was going to join her then he apparently changed his mind, opting to walk across to perch his hips on the edge of the window-sill.

Well, he couldn't get much further away from me, she thought uneasily. Not unless he's going to climb out of the window.

The silence stretched and grew until it almost took on a solid identity of its own between them before he spoke.

'Freya, I know I was the one who suggested this

marriage,' he began uncomfortably, and her heart plummeted.

Was he going to suggest an annulment straight away? That was something she hadn't expected. The baby wasn't due for another four months and...

'But I hope we have enough regard for each other...' He paused and shook his head, clearly disgusted. 'Listen to me, I sound like some mealy-mouthed guidance counsellor. What I'm trying to say is, if I ask you a question, will you answer honestly?'

For a moment cowardice nearly won. With that sort of build-up, what sort of question was coming? But she wasn't the sort of person who let fear rule her and already her brain was starting to work at high speed. If Finn wanted a guarantee of honesty, perhaps she could take advantage and level the playing field a bit.

'Only if you return the favour,' she challenged, suddenly conscious that she'd tipped her chin up in the air in the way she always did when she was fighting her corner, and that he'd noticed. 'Question for question?'

'Deal,' he confirmed. 'Do you want to go first?'

'What a gentleman,' she said with a swift and probably noticeably insincere grin. 'But as it was your idea, you go first.'

'OK.' She saw his chest expand with the deep breath he drew and suddenly wondered just how nervous he was about this confrontation. If their arrange-

ment meant nothing more to him than that—an arrangement—and if he didn't care for her any more
than he did for any other relative by marriage, surely
it wouldn't matter that much to him.

As it was, there was an intensity to his expression
that she hadn't seen since...since that night five
months ago. Her heart began to thump. If he asked
her right out whether she loved him...

When he finally spoke she couldn't believe her
ears.

'Do you still love Colum?' he demanded bluntly,
both hands curved so tightly around the edge of the
window-sill that his knuckles were white.

'Do I *what*!' she gasped. It was a good job she was
sitting down or she'd have fallen over with the shock
of it. Whatever question she'd been expecting, it
hadn't been that. Why on earth would Finn ask such
a thing unless...?

Anger struck just a split second after the realisation
of the significance of the question. He actually
thought...

'Of course I love him...as a *brother-in-law*,' she
said heavily. 'And if you think I would for one moment do anything to jeopardise my sister's happiness
by fooling around with Colum, you need your
head—'

'Freya, no!' Finn exclaimed, hurriedly breaking
into her tirade. 'That's not what I meant at all. I *know*
you wouldn't want to hurt Astrid or the boys, but I

also know that you were in love with him first…with Colum, I mean. The rest of the family doesn't know that, but they *do* know that you haven't bothered much with dating over the last six years and—'

'And you presumed that you knew why,' she accused heatedly, all sorts of unwelcome thoughts now whirling inside her head.

She knew her mother had been campaigning for more grandchildren and had been gently trying to nudge her towards marriage, but she'd also admitted after the ceremony that she'd known for a long time about Freya's love for Finn.

Finn was a different matter entirely and a very confusing one.

If he believed that she was in love with Colum, why on earth had he offered to marry her? Surely concern for her mother couldn't have been the only reason?

'Freya, help me out here,' he demanded, breaking into her whirling thoughts and looking uncharacteristically frazzled. 'I know you're not the type to go in for one-night stands and we all know you haven't had any sort of steady boyfriend, at least in the last year, that I know of, so who the hell *is* the baby's father?'

Well, at least he knew she was basically a moral person, but Colum had been right to tell her she'd need to be patient with him.

Was the man blind? How could he not have seen what had been going on under his nose for six years?

'What do you mean? *What's* been going on?' he snapped, and she suddenly realised that she'd actually spoken her thoughts aloud.

Well, she mused swiftly, perhaps shock tactics *would* work best.

'Oh, nothing much,' she said airily. 'Just the fact that the reason why I haven't dated much is that I've been in love with *you* for six years.'

'You've *what*?' he exploded, coming off the window-sill as though catapulted into orbit, only to come to a halt in the middle of the room. 'Oh, no, you haven't. You've avoided me every chance you've had, treated me like a leper if I got within ten feet.' There was genuine hurt in his voice at the end but she knew that was easily dismissed.

'Only because I couldn't trust myself any closer,' she said softly, her heart beating loudly as she finally made the admission. She was risking a great deal, but there was so much to be won if he could only admit that he cared enough to try to make theirs a real marriage.

'You always treated me like a sister, and a nuisance of a younger sister at that,' she continued when he seemed unable, or unwilling, to comment. 'You didn't want to know that just being in the same room with you scrambled my brain and threatened me with cardiac failure.'

'You stupid woman!' he exclaimed as he strode across the room, and hauled her out of the settee and into his arms. 'I've spent six years waiting for just one clue that your heart was beating as fast as mine. Six years and a million gallons of cold-water showers.' And then he was kissing her as though determined to make up for every one of those years.

Freya's head was spinning. With his arms wrapped so tightly around her, her feet didn't even reach the floor, but that didn't matter. She had no intention of going anywhere, not when this was where she had wanted to be ever since she'd met Finn.

A whole new world had been born by the time he slowly lifted his head. It was as though even then he was reluctant to breathe when he could have been kissing instead.

'Ah, Freya, what a pair of idiots we've been,' he groaned with his forehead pressed against hers. 'I've spent six years, ever since that foursome when Colum fell for Astrid like a ton of bricks, waiting for you to start dating again so I'd know you were ready to move on from him.'

'It was never going to happen because it wasn't Colum I was in love with,' she finished. 'What on earth made you think I was?'

'Colum himself,' Finn said as he settled himself into his favourite leather recliner with Freya tucked firmly in his arms. 'When he invited me to join the foursome he said he'd met a woman who made him want to settle down.'

'Then he met Astrid and knew he'd *really* met his match. But, Finn, as far as I was concerned, he was just a really nice man, the sort I would have liked to have had as an older brother. We got on well but there wasn't that spark…that awareness…' It was difficult to find the words she wanted when she was close enough to hear Finn's heart beating, close enough to see the many different greens and golds that went to make up his fascinating eyes.

'Freya…' he whispered huskily, 'if you keep looking at me like that we'll never finish this conversation.'

'I thought we'd finished the talking part,' she complained distractedly, wanting nothing more than to take up the kissing where they'd left off. As Finn had said, they had time to make up for.

'But you didn't answer the question,' he insisted seriously as he grabbed her hand to stop her playing with the buttons on his shirt.

'I did. I told you I'm not in love with Colum, I'm in love with *you*…and you haven't told me the same,' she grumbled.

'Of course I've said I love you…haven't I?'

She shook her head, fighting a grin when she saw him realise that she was going to insist.

'You're wrong, Freya,' he said softly. 'If you think I don't want to say the words, you couldn't be more wrong. I nearly blurted them out when I proposed, but I was afraid it would frighten you off. They've been burning a hole in my tongue for years and the only times I've been able to use them is in my dreams.'

'You dream about me?' The thought was infinitely enticing, especially if they were the sort of dreams that involved declarations of love.

'Yes. Constantly. Wicked ones,' he admitted with an equally wicked grin that set her pulse racing and started desire coiling deep inside her.

There was nothing she could do to curb the feelings, but her ingrained sense of honesty was telling her that it was time to reveal her last secret. Finn had a right to know.

'They've been especially vivid over the last few months,' he continued in a husky voice, his eyes darkly intent as they began to roam over her. 'Since that conference in Paris, in fact. Perhaps there was something in the air?'

Freya was suddenly sidetracked from her good intentions, unable to believe what she was hearing.

He'd been having wicked dreams ever since that trip? Dreams about her?

For the first time she wondered whether the drug Finn had been given might not have been totally efficient at blanking out his memory. She knew it was fairly quickly eliminated from the body, and if he'd only been given a minimum dose... Was it possible that some of the events of those few hours might not be buried quite so deeply in his subconscious?

Then she saw his expression change and she knew that he'd reached the end of the line, too. It was time for that one last question. All she could do was pray that he believed her and accepted the answer. She held her breath and waited.

'Freya...' he began softly, obviously searching for the words he wanted, and she decided to give him all the space he needed, especially when he curved his hand protectively over the gentle swell of her unborn child. 'Now that you know I love you,' he continued, 'I hope you also know that I'll love your child...even children, should they come along. So, will you tell me about the father of this little one?'

When the question finally emerged it did so in a rush, almost as though he hated to have to ask and dreaded the answer.

'Oh, Finn, if your dreams started after that trip to Paris, then you must already know all about him. He's the only man in the world that I've ever loved—the only one I've ever made love with.'

It took a moment for the penny to drop but when she saw the way his eyes widened and darkened then flew down to gaze at the curve of her belly under his hand she felt tears gathering behind her eyes.

He stroked her gently, almost as though trying to communicate with the tiny being covered by his hand.

'Mine?' he whispered in amazement, his eyes

brighter too as he gave an exultant laugh. 'That's *my* baby in there? Oh, Freya, why didn't you say something sooner? I've missed so many months of the pregnancy.'

There was that element of pain again and she hurried to explain.

'I didn't do it to hurt you deliberately,' she promised, cupping his freshly shaven jaw in her hand. 'But I had no way of knowing about the seasickness or the injection so I had no idea about the amnesia. When you never mentioned what had happened on the ferry and actually seemed to want to continue being nothing more than a friend, I thought it meant you didn't want any more of me than you'd had.'

'You thought I'd treat you as a one-night stand?' he demanded angrily, glaring down at her from just inches away. 'When have you ever seen me treat a woman like that?'

'Don't be angry, Finn. I really didn't know what to think when you never said a single word, never made a sign that there had ever been anything intimate between us.' She sent up a silent prayer that she was doing a good enough job of explaining. She couldn't bear it if everything were to fall apart now.

'But what about when you found out about the baby? Why didn't you say something then?'

'Because I loved you and I didn't want you to marry me unless you felt the same way,' she said resolutely. 'I love my mother and I wouldn't want to hurt her, but I certainly didn't want to be married just because of the baby.'

'Well, that's certainly ironic, considering that's what you ended up doing.' Finn laughed, but there was no humour or delight in the sound this time. 'So what were you planning to do with the baby when it arrived? Give it up for adoption? Hide it away with a babysitter when you visited your family?'

'I honestly don't know, Finn. I hadn't got that far,' she admitted miserably. 'I couldn't face telling you and I was living in dread of the first time somebody realised I was pregnant, and then—'

'And then your mother needed surgery,' he finished for her. 'And your options narrowed down to almost nothing.'

He gave a heavy sigh and was silent for so long that Freya decided it was time she got off his lap.

'Where do you think you're going?' he demanded softly, his arms tightening around her just enough to let her know that she wasn't going anywhere.

'Well, I just thought you might need a bit of space while you think about everything,' she offered uncertainly, suddenly less sure of his reaction than she'd thought she'd be.

'The sort of things I need to think about are far easier if I've got you right where you are,' he said firmly, pressing her head to his shoulder. 'You know, our lives would probably have run a lot smoother if our families had got involved in this.'

'Involved in what?' Freya had obviously lost the thread when he'd refused to let her go.

'In how things ended up,' he said. 'There we are, two reasonably intelligent people bumping into each other regularly because our two families have been joined by marriage and then ending up working together day after day. We're eating our hearts out for each other and don't do anything about it until I'm zapped with an anti-emetic. It sounds like a bad plot line for one of those daytime soaps.'

She smiled up at him. 'I suppose we were so intent on hiding our own feelings that we couldn't see what was in front of our noses. But everyone else in the family seemed to know how we felt. Certainly your brother and my mother.'

He tucked her head comfortably under his chin and she revelled in the possessive way she was completely enfolded by his much bigger body. It was such bliss to be this close to Finn again, but it would be even better if there weren't quite so many layers between them.

'Freya, I've been thinking,' Finn said slowly, his deep voice a dark rumble against her ear and infinitely sexy. 'Those dreams I've been having…do you suppose they might actually be memories?'

She tilted her head back to look up at him again, and was fascinated to see the wash of colour heightening his face.

'Well, if you only had a partial dose, it's possible,

but that would depend what happens in the dreams,' she said softly, suddenly finding the role of seductress much easier to slip into than she'd thought. 'For example, do they start with a shower?'

Perhaps her fright with the hairy intruder today was actually going to be of benefit if it helped to jog his memory.

He groaned and she knew she was on the right track.

'And was I naked when you came in and all wet because I didn't know that the control was stuck on cold and I shrieked and leapt out?'

He groaned again and then struggled his way out of the soft upholstery without letting go of her.

'I'll tell you what,' he said as he carried her towards the bathroom, 'let's see if we can re-enact the whole thing. Perhaps that will bring it all back to me.'

He kicked the door shut behind him and leant back against it before he lowered her feet to the floor.

'Now, where were we?' he mused as nimble fingers parted buttons from buttonholes at record speed and his shirt hit the floor. 'In my dream you're completely naked and I'm just wearing…'

'How about skipping a couple of stages?' she suggested as she pulled the silky tunic up over her head and reached for the drawstring at her waist. Just the sight of that broad muscular chest was enough to double her pulse and make her impatient for the pleasures she remembered only too well. 'Let's fast-forward to where I helped you out of your trousers and you—'

'Hey! Slow down! We don't want to rush anything or we might miss something important,' he complained as he began to explore the silky skin she'd already bared.

'That would be a shame,' she agreed breathlessly, undeterred as she unzipped him and pulled the rest of his clothes down. 'Then we'd have to start all over again until we get it right.'

'Hmm, you're right,' he said as he lifted her up onto the edge of the vanity unit and parted her knees to step between them. 'We might have to do this over and over again until it's absolutely perfect.'

Freya automatically wrapped her arms around his neck and locked her heels behind his back even while she was tilting her head to invite his kisses.

The first time this had happened he'd had to show her what to do. This time she knew just what would bring them both pleasure and couldn't wait for it to begin.

At the very last moment Finn paused to stare down into her eyes.

'I love you, Freya Wylie,' he declared, his deep voice giving the words an extra resonance that coiled warmly around her heart.

He stroked her hair away from her face with a tender hand, and when he traced a long dark spiral as it draped over her shoulder and across her breast she was glad she'd left it loose the way he liked it.

'Six years,' he whispered as he bent to allow his lips to follow his fingertip. 'Six years of loving you and longing for you and hiding it behind smiles. And if you hadn't needed an emergency groom...'

'Shh,' she said softly, unwinding an arm to place one finger on his lips then following it with her own lips for a tender kiss. 'Those six years weren't wasted. They gave our love time to grow while we were working on our careers. Now we're ready to reap the benefits. Anyway,' she added with a brief kiss to silence him when he would have spoken, 'there's a very serious scientific experiment going on here. We're not just trying to find out what level of memories are recoverable after that anti-emetic, we're also turning an emergency groom into a long-term lover and husband.'

'A scientific experiment, Dr Wylie? How long do you think that's going to take?' he demanded on a groan when she tightened her arms around him and slid her body sensually against his.

'Oh, I'm not sure, Dr Wylie. At a guess it's going to take at least the next fifty or sixty years, if we work really hard at it.' It was beginning to get very difficult to concentrate when he was exploring her curves like that.

'Fifty or sixty? Well, then,' he said with a wicked

grin as he angled his head ready to kiss her again, those fascinating green eyes gleaming down at her with a lifetime of love, 'in that case we'd better not waste any more time.'

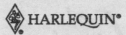

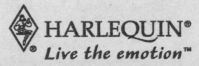

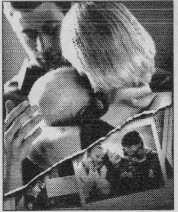
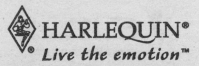

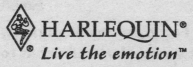